# DORK
## IN DISGUISE

# DORK
## IN DISGUISE

# Carol Gorman

■ HarperCollins*Publishers*

Library of Congress Cataloging-in-Publication Data
Gorman, Carol.
    Dork in disguise / Carol Gorman.
        p.    cm.
    Summary: Starting middle school in a new town, brainy Jerry Flack changes
his image from "dork" to "cool kid," only to discover that he'd rather be himself.
    ISBN 0-06-024866-1. — ISBN 0-06-024867-X (lib. bdg.)
    [1. Self-acceptance—Fiction.   2. Popularity—Fiction.   3. Moving, Household—
Fiction.   4. Schools—Fiction.]   I. Title.
PZ7.G6693Do   1999                                                    99-27898
[Fic]—dc21                                                                CIP

Typography by Hilary Zarycky
1   2   3   4   5   6   7   8   9   10
❖
First Edition

## ACKNOWLEDGMENTS

I'd like to thank Sara and Nicole Mallie, Katie Simpson, Katrina Reschley and Mrs. Cindy McDonald's sixth grade language arts class at Taft Middle School for their help with this book.

A special thanks goes to Mr. Al Covington, sixth grade science teacher at Harding Middle School.

I couldn't have written this book without the generous help of Mr. Doug Nauman, physics teacher at Washington High School, who not only showed me how he built a hovercraft, he gave me a ride on it! Mr. Nauman also read the manuscript and made invaluable suggestions. Any errors in the science content were mine alone.

And finally, a fond thank you to Susan Rich—one of the best editors in this business—who constantly impresses me with her hard work, dedication, and delightful ideas.

Carol Gorman
Cedar Rapids, Iowa

*To my niece and nephews,*
*Alicia, Brandon, and Alex Maxwell*

# Chapter One

"You can let me out here," Jerry Flack said to his mother.

It was the first day of school, and the oatmeal Jerry had eaten for breakfast lay like a brick in his stomach.

"But your school is still three blocks away," his mother said. She slowed the car to avoid hitting a squirrel that darted across the road.

"That's okay," Jerry said. "I'll walk to school starting tomorrow. I measured the distance on my bike odometer, and it's only seven-tenths of a mile. At a rate of three and a half miles an hour, I should be able to get to school in . . ." He paused, staring up at the sun visor, and figured it out. "In about twelve minutes."

Then he realized he was doing it again—figuring math problems in his head. Something only a dork would do. It was a good thing there wasn't anyone around.

After all, this was the first day at a new school, in a new town, and Jerry was turning over a new leaf. This was the first day of the rest of his life.

He had a plan all worked out. He was going to stop being a brain, a dork. He would start Nathaniel Hawthorne Middle School disguised as a Cool Guy.

He'd used styling gel on his hair this morning before he blew his hair dry. The gel had worked its magic. His hair didn't stick out the way it usually did. And it was "full of body," just as the label had promised.

But Jerry knew that being cool wasn't just about hair. It was more, so much more. He had studied the subject for several months now, ever since his parents had said they were moving to Spencer Lake. He had pored for hours over magazines like *Teen Scene* and *Ultimate Cool* and gossip magazines like *Guess Who?* and *Dishin' Dirt*. He had watched endless hours of music videos on TV and had lurked in plenty of teen chat rooms on the Web, trying to get a feel for how cool kids talked to one another.

But the subject of cool was broad and deep, and

Jerry wondered whether he knew enough for his disguise to work. How things went today would tell him a lot about whether he had prepared himself sufficiently.

"Just pull up at the corner," Jerry said.

His mother stopped the car. "Remember to go straight home after school and stay with Melissa. I'll be back after my four o'clock class."

"Okay," Jerry said.

"Have a good day, kiddo."

"Thanks." Jerry was glad no one heard his mother call him "kiddo," and he made a mental note never to let his mother near other kids. Cool Guys don't have mothers who call them cute names.

He got out of the car. "Bye, Mom." He shut the door and watched her drive away.

When she was safely out of view, he took off his glasses and poked them into his backpack. The world around him looked a little blurry. He could see fuzzy cars sweep past, a couple of cloudy kids on bikes, and a smeary dog barking in the next yard. That was okay. He could get used to it. Cool Guys didn't wear glasses.

He strolled along the sidewalk for the next three blocks. It was a good thing there had been a sale on T-shirts that weekend. He'd left his "World's Best Grandson" shirt in his closet (and planned to throw it in the garbage sometime soon when his mother wasn't looking) and put on his new Vikings shirt.

He didn't know very much about the Vikings, except that they were a football team in Minnesota. That was a subject he planned on looking into when he had more time. Cool Guys knew about sports.

The grounds around the school were crowded. He stopped next to an oak tree and leaned against it. He didn't think a Cool Guy would walk right up to strangers and start a conversation. It would be better to hang back a bit to get a feel for the place.

A couple of guys chased each other around the flagpole, laughing. Definitely not cool, Jerry thought.

To his right, three girls—all blond—stood together, flipping their long hair over their shoulders.

"What a summer I had," said Blonde Number One. "The best summer of my life."

"All because of Adam," Blonde Number Two said knowingly.

Blonde Number Three nodded sadly. "I can't believe his family has to move," she said. "Will you keep in touch with him?"

"We promised to e-mail every single day," Blonde Number One said.

Blondes Number Two and Three sighed. "That's so romantic," Three said.

These girls were unquestionably cool, Jerry thought, but too old for him. They were very tall, probably eighth graders.

A guy came rollerblading past, followed by another guy on skates. They looked like they'd been skating all their lives, the way they threaded their way around the kids who stood like plastic cones on an obstacle course. The kid skating in front wore a red Adidas shirt. He ran both hands through his thick, wavy hair as he glided past. Jerry stared at him. The guy oozed cool from every pore.

The kids in the crowd all turned to look at them.

"Those guys are from Frost Elementary," Jerry heard one girl whisper to her friend. "The hunk in front is Gabe Marshall."

"He's *gorgeous*," said the friend, who was tall and good-looking herself. "You suppose I could go with a sixth grader?"

"No way," the first girl said. "Seventh-grade girls don't go with sixth-grade guys. In fact, they hardly *look* at them."

Out of the corner of Jerry's eye, a blurry figure appeared and a scent of spicy perfume wafted past his nose. He turned to look and gulped. She was the most beautiful girl he had seen in his entire life. Flowing, dark red hair tumbled down the middle of her back. She had a small, heart-shaped face and a button nose, and like the others, she was watching Gabe and his friend, who were still rollerblading in big figure eights through the crowd.

"He's my goal for this year," the beautiful girl said. "The one in front. He's so *cool*."

"If anyone can get him, it's you, Cinnamon," her friend said.

"Think so?" Cinnamon smiled, still staring at Gabe.

"Let's play our game," the friend said eagerly. "What would you give up for him?"

Cinnamon giggled. "Uh—I'd give up a semester of TV."

"Wow."

"How about you?" Cinnamon asked.

"Hmm. I'd give up pizza for a month."

"Only a month?" Cinnamon asked.

"Hey, he's *really* cool," her friend said, "but pizza's my favorite food."

Cinnamon laughed, and they strolled on past.

A voice right next to Jerry startled him. "Why don't you put on your glasses?" He turned to see a girl staring at him.

"Hunh?" he said. "What do you mean? What glasses?"

"The ones you were wearing this morning," she said.

"How did you know?"

"You're squinting," she explained. "And you have little dents on either side of your nose. You took off your glasses less than an hour ago. Maybe a half hour."

Jerry was impressed. He looked at her more closely. She was average height with brown hair that turned under just above her shoulders. A pair of red glasses perched on her nose.

"I don't like wearing glasses," he said.

"Tell me about it," she said. "They're uncomfortable, they fall down your nose if they don't fit right, and they make you look like a dork." She gazed at him curiously. "Trying to change your image?"

Jerry was astounded. Could this girl read his mind?

"What did you say your name was?" she asked.

"I didn't," Jerry said. "But it's Jerry Flack."

The girl put out her hand. "Brenda McAdams."

Jerry shook her hand, hoping no one was watching. He was pretty sure that Cool Guys didn't shake hands with girls. He'd only been on the school grounds for a few minutes, and already he was doing something dorky.

"Nice to meet you, Jerry," she said. "You new in town?"

"Yeah," Jerry said.

"That's what I figured, that you're starting out fresh in Spencer Lake with a new image. Are your parents with the university?"

Jerry glanced over his shoulder to see if anyone was listening. He didn't want people overhearing what she said, because she was so right about him. No one seemed to be paying attention, though.

"Yes."

"You're in sixth grade?" Brenda asked.

"Yeah. You too?"

"Yes indeedy," Brenda said. She seemed to study him closely. "Well, Jerry, if you want to change your image, there are still some things you'll need to do."

Jerry rolled his eyes. He didn't need a *girl* telling him how to be cool. Especially *this* girl, who clearly wasn't cool herself. Nobody cool says "yes indeedy."

"I'm doing okay," Jerry said, turning to go.

"I saw you watching Cinnamon O'Brien," Brenda said, stopping Jerry in his tracks.

"Do you know her?" he asked, turning back to her.

Brenda nodded. "She was in my class at Hemingway Elementary. You hear her talking about that kid on rollerblades? Isn't it interesting how the good-looking kids all gravitate to each other in the first few minutes of the school year? Even though they come from at least five different elementary schools, I bet by the end of the day all the 'beautiful people' will be best friends."

"So . . . what's she like?" Jerry asked.

"Cinnamon? Dumb."

"What else?"

Brenda laughed. "I tell you she's an airhead, and you want to know more?"

"There are worse things than being . . . less than a genius."

Brenda smiled. "Like being uncool?"

Jerry decided to ignore that. "Are you and Cinnamon friends?"

"Depends what you mean by 'friends.' I don't hang out with her, but I don't hate her or anything. You want to meet her? I'll introduce you."

Jerry's heart began to race. "Uh, yeah. But not right now."

"Why not?"

"I'm . . . not ready."

Brenda stood back and looked at him critically. "Yes, you could use some coaching."

Jerry scowled. "Hey, leave me alone, will you? I don't need your help."

Brenda shrugged. "Whatever you say. Just thought I could be of assistance."

She walked away as the bell rang.

Jerry was shaken. This girl had seen through him right away. He wondered if there were other kids who would know immediately that his Cool Guy image was a disguise.

He'd have to study the fine points of coolness, Jerry thought. Maybe he'd missed a few important details.

Jerry watched the blurry mass of strangers around him and thought about what his life had been like at his old school. He'd been a dork with only a couple of close friends, and they also scored pretty high on the Dorkometer. But this is a new year, Jerry thought. If he could learn all the finer points of coolness, maybe he could get Cinnamon to notice him.

Maybe she'd even *speak* to him sometime. Not just "Sorry," or "Excuse me," for bumping into him in a crowded hall—although Jerry thought bumping into Cinnamon would be extremely pleasant.

Jerry was thinking how wonderful it would be if she'd look him in the eyes, smile, and say "Hi."

It would even be cooler if she said his name along with the "Hi."

*"Hi, Jerry."*

That would be unbelievably cool.

He reached the school door. This is it, he thought. His first day. He'd have to be more careful so other kids wouldn't see through his disguise.

He could do it, he reassured himself. He'd just have to be on guard every moment.

# Chapter Two

Jerry walked down the corridor on the ground floor and squinted up at the room numbers as he passed. The registration materials that had come in the mail said that his homeroom was room 112 with Mrs. Barnaby.

He found the classroom and walked in. The seats were nearly all taken, but Jerry found a desk near the back. The teacher leaned against her desk and chatted with some girls in the front seats.

"Okay, folks," the woman said after the bell rang. "This is homeroom, and I'm Mrs. Barnaby. Are you all in the right place?" No one said they weren't, so she continued. "Let's see who's here."

She took roll, then handed everyone their class

schedules and locker assignments. "You'll each have a partner," she said. "Now, if you'll follow me, we'll go to our locker area down the hall, and you can practice opening your lockers. If you have any trouble, ask me for help. If not, come on back here when you're done and wait for the others."

Mrs. Barnaby led everyone down the hall. Jerry's was the locker on the very end.

A blond kid stood there, turning the combination lock.

"Hi," Jerry said. "You got locker one hundred, too?"

The kid looked at him. "Yeah. I guess we're sharing it." He opened the door. Inside were two shelves and two coat hooks.

"You want the top shelf or bottom?" Jerry asked.

The kid shrugged and leaned against the wall next to the locker. "I don't care."

Jerry realized that a Cool Guy wouldn't care which shelf he had. "Me either," he said.

"Well, we got it open. Mission accomplished." The kid stared at him with clear blue eyes. "So you got a name?"

"Jerry." Jerry had a feeling it might be cooler just to give his first name. That's the way it went in some cool teen horror movies he'd rented this summer.

"I'm Craig."

"So, you want to go back?" Jerry asked.

"What I want is to liven up this party, man," Craig said.

"What do you mean?"

"I mean, I want to stir things up. See some action." Craig smirked. "Follow me."

Jerry's instincts told him to stay put. But he knew if he did that, he'd blow his cover. Craig would think he was a dork.

So Jerry followed him, and to his surprise, Craig walked back to their homeroom. They were the first people to return; the room was empty.

"Come on," Craig said. "We've got to work fast."

"What are we doing?"

Craig picked up a desk and turned it upside down. "This. Hurry, before somebody comes."

Jerry stared at him. Was he kidding?

Jerry wished he could just turn around and leave. But how could he risk looking like a wimp? He figured he'd better play along. He shrugged, picked up the nearest desk, and set it down on its side.

Craig kicked over the wastebasket and turned over Mrs. Barnaby's chair. He picked up papers on her desk and tore them in half and threw them on the floor. Then he wrote with chalk on the board: *The Fantom Tornado Strikes!*

Jerry opened his mouth to tell Craig he'd misspelled *Phantom*, then realized a Cool Guy might not care how to spell it. He closed his mouth again.

In a half minute, the room was a disaster. Jerry began to sweat as he took in the damage. Half the desks were toppled over, and everything that had been piled on them was strewn on the floor. A mug full of pencils from Mrs. Barnaby's desk and all the erasers from the blackboards had been tossed around the room. Wood shavings from the pencil sharpener were scattered across the floor like confetti.

"One last thing," Craig said. To Jerry's amazement, he opened Mrs. Barnaby's desk drawer and pulled out a box of tacks. He turned it over, and the tacks rained down on Mrs. Barnaby's desk, her overturned chair, and the floor.

Jerry wished he had done anything other than come back with this maniac. Turning over a chair or two was one thing, but this was vandalism, pure and simple.

Craig ran back to the middle of the room just as the first four students returned.

"Gee, what happened?" said a pony-tailed girl, stopping in the doorway.

"Wow!" her friend said. The other two kids surveyed the damage with their mouths open.

Jerry's locker partner plastered an innocent look on his face. "It was like this when we walked in. Right?" He looked at Jerry.

"Uh, yeah," Jerry said. He could feel the heat rising in his face. He knew that turning red would give him away, but he couldn't stop it.

Jerry picked up his own desk and set it upright. Then he sat down.

"Look at the board," the pony-tailed girl said.

Her friend made a face. "What an idiot. He couldn't even spell *phantom* right."

"I'm getting Mrs. Barnaby," the pony-tailed girl said. She disappeared into the hall.

Craig shot Jerry a grin. Jerry didn't smile back.

Within a minute, Mrs. Barnaby stopped in the doorway, gawking. "Who did this?" she demanded.

"It was like this when we got back from our lockers," Craig said.

"What's your name?" she asked him, walking into the room.

"Craig Fox," he said. "I was with my locker partner." He pointed at Jerry.

"And you are—?"

Jerry had to clear his throat before his voice would work. "Jerry Flack."

Mrs. Barnaby sent a girl to get the assistant principal. "This is outrageous," she said. "Everybody pick up your desks."

The bell rang, and Mrs. Barnaby said, "You all must go to your first-period class now. Craig and Jerry, Mr. Meyer may send for you later." Jerry wondered if she knew the truth.

Jerry got up and moved with the rest of the kids into the hall. He hurried away, hoping to avoid

Craig, and climbed the stairs to his language arts class.

Knowing he'd need to sit fairly close to see the blackboard, he picked the second seat in the middle row.

Still shaken by the incident downstairs, he kept half an eye on the door, hoping that Craig wouldn't be in this class.

One by one the students came in and sat down. Jerry began to relax when the room was nearly full, and Craig hadn't come in. His stomach executed a cartwheel, though, when Cinnamon O'Brien arrived. She took a seat in the back and began whispering to a girl who sat next to her. Gabe Marshall walked in, and Jerry heard giggles from the girls in the back.

Brenda McAdams was the last student to arrive. She plopped down in the last empty seat, right in front of Jerry.

"Hi, Flack," she said.

"Hi."

It was good to see Brenda. After the episode with Craig, Jerry was relieved to talk to someone who wasn't interested in making trouble.

Brenda leaned closer and murmured out the side of her mouth, "Smart move, sitting close so you can see without your glasses." She gazed over Jerry's shoulder. "Guess who's sitting in the back? Cinnamon O'Brien."

Jerry winced. He didn't want to talk to Brenda about Cinnamon now, when other kids might overhear. He was glad when the teacher walked in from the hall, and Brenda turned to face the front of the room.

"Good morning, everyone. I'm Ms. Robertson, and this is period one, language arts class. We'll all stay together for second-period social studies, too."

Ms. Robertson was pretty and small, not much bigger than Jerry. He had a hard time believing she was old enough to be a teacher.

Ms. Robertson took roll and then told them about the stories and novels they would read and the papers they would write this year. She had a beautiful singing kind of voice—nice, with lots of highs and lows.

"I'd like us all to get to know one another," Ms. Robertson said. She handed papers to the first people in each row. "Pass them back, please. These sheets have some fun questions. Fill in the answers, and then we'll divide into small groups and introduce ourselves."

When Jerry got his sheet, he looked down the list of questions. The first ones were easy: name, family members, pets. Then came the rest:

*If you could be a person from history, who would you be?*

*What is the craziest thing you've ever done?*

*What's the funniest thing you've ever done?*

Jerry knew he'd have to be careful on this questionnaire. One slip, and everyone would know he wasn't cool.

He took out a No. 2 pencil, freshly sharpened that morning, and set to work. The first three questions were no problem. Then came the harder ones.

A person in history, Jerry thought. Who was really cool—and dead? George Washington or Thomas Edison or Albert Einstein? None of those guys would score points with the cool kids.

Jerry wrote, *Elvis Presley.*

*What is the craziest thing you've ever done?* Jerry wasn't sure he'd ever done anything crazy, so he'd have to make up something. He thought a minute, then wrote: *I went hang gliding with my dog.*

Not bad. It had an element of danger, plus it was kind of cool that he took his dog along.

The funniest thing he'd ever done? Hmmm. Jerry usually didn't do things that were very funny. He'd have to make this one up, too.

After half a minute of thinking, he wrote: *Once I met a famous football player, and I told him a joke that really cracked him up!*

No, that wouldn't work, Jerry thought. The kids would want to know *which* famous football player, and Jerry didn't know of any.

So Jerry erased *a famous football player* and wrote *Leonardo DiCaprio.* He had a joke all ready to tell in case anyone asked what he'd said to Leo.

Jerry sat back and read over his answers. He'd done a good job. If he didn't know otherwise, he'd assume this was written by a Cool Guy with a very exciting life.

After a few more minutes, Ms. Robertson divided the class into four groups. Jerry's group met in the back of the room and included Brenda, Cinnamon, and the girl Cinnamon had whispered to before class started.

"Switch papers with the person next to you," said Ms. Robertson, "and introduce your partner to the group."

Jerry's partner turned out to be Cinnamon's friend. Her name was Robin Hedges. He looked at her paper. She had some good answers, but they paled in comparison to his.

Meanwhile, Robin was reading Jerry's paper. Her eyes widened as she looked up at him. "You really met Leonardo DiCaprio? *Cool!*"

"Yeah, well . . ." Jerry smiled modestly. He was off to a great start.

When it was time to introduce their partners, Jerry's stomach filled with butterflies. He was going to have to introduce Robin, and Cinnamon would be watching him. He'd have to be careful. *You only get one chance to make a first impression.* He'd read that somewhere, and its meaning loomed large in his mind.

Brenda was first. She introduced a guy named

Scott Perkins who said he'd be Abraham Lincoln from history, that he'd once entered a crazy frog-jumping contest, and the funniest thing he'd ever done was write *Wash me, you dirty scumbag* on someone's filthy car.

Scott introduced Brenda, who said she'd be the scientist Madame Curie from history. The craziest thing she'd ever done was dress as a flapper for Halloween, and her funniest experience was trying to wake up her sister when she was so sound asleep, she *wouldn't* wake up.

"That was funny?" Robin asked, frowning.

"Yeah," Brenda said. "See, she was just like this rag doll, a floppy deadweight. I couldn't stop laughing."

Robin rolled her eyes at Cinnamon, who grinned back at her.

Everyone in the group took turns until only Jerry and Robin and Cinnamon and her partner were left.

Robin introduced Jerry. When she read that Jerry went hang gliding with his dog, Cinnamon laughed. Then Robin read his answer to the last question. Cinnamon gasped, "You *met* Leonardo DiCaprio? What did you say to make him laugh?"

Jerry's heart stopped for a moment. *Cinnamon had spoken to him.* Twelve whole words, and they were now indelibly stamped on his brain. He'd remember them forever.

Abruptly, Jerry realized those words had formed two questions, and Cinnamon was waiting for an answer.

His heart started again; it was now pounding away in his chest. His fingers tingled. Jerry glanced down at his hands and stared at them in horror. His fingernails and knuckles glowed white; he had the edge of his desk in a death grip. He dropped his hands into his lap.

"Uh, well—" *Think!* he hollered silently at himself. He scanned his memory for details from his Cool research.

"I was playing in a band at a Fourth of July celebration, and Leo was making a movie nearby, and he stopped to listen. He came over and talked to me after we played our set." It was a great lie, considering his brain was whirring out of control, like a windmill in a tornado.

"Cool!" Cinnamon said. "What was the funny story?"

"Uh—" Jerry faltered. What was it? His mind went blank! He'd just thought of it a second ago.

"Oh, okay, I got it now," he said. "What do you get when you cross a doberman with a Lassie-dog?"

"What?" Cinnamon asked, grinning.

"Uh." Jerry faltered. *What was the punchline?* He was so nervous!

Come on, brain! *What was it?*

"So *what* already?" asked Robin, frowning. "You

mean you can't even remember it?"

"I—I'll think of it in a second," he said meekly. "Oh yeah." He laughed with relief. "I remember now. What do you get when you cross a doberman with a Lassie-dog? A dog that bites you in the leg, then runs and gets help."

But his timing had been really bad, and timing was important with jokes. Brenda laughed heartily, but the others only smiled.

Robin was obviously unimpressed. "Okay, now you introduce me," she ordered.

Jerry had to do better this time. *Much* better. His future was hanging in the balance.

"Uh, this is Robin Hedges," Jerry said, pointing at her with his thumb. "She has two sisters and a cat named Ralph. She'd be Marilyn Monroe from history." Jerry stopped and looked at her, his heart racing, and decided to risk making a snappy comment. "Yeah, Monroe was the epitome of *cool*."

The word was out of his mouth before he could stop it.

"Uh-pit-uh-me?" Robin said scornfully. "What's that?"

"She was real cool," Jerry said lamely in a small voice. He felt the heat spread across his face. He stared at Robin's paper and read the rest in a fast jumble. "Robin-was-a-flower-girl-in-her-aunt's-wedding-when-she-was-three-and-she-danced-all-the-way-down-the-aisle-because-she-liked-the-music-and-she-put-salt-in-the-sugar-bowl-at-home-and-her-dad-drank-his-coffee-and-spit-it-out-all-over-the-table."

Jerry didn't look up, but he heard a few giggles. Robin frowned. "Could you understand what he said?"

"What about the coffee?" asked Cinnamon.

Robin answered slowly, with distinctly pronounced words, "I put salt in the sugar bowl, and my dad drank his coffee and spit it out all over the table."

"Ha!" Cinnamon said. "That's funny."

Jerry looked at the floor. He'd been about as uncool as a guy could get. His head began to fill with all the clever comments he could have made after reading Robin's comment that she'd be Marilyn Monroe from history.

For instance, he could've looked her right in the eye and said in his lowest, sexiest voice, "Well, if I'm Elvis Presley, we could make a really cool pair."

Or maybe being funny would've been better. He could've pretended to stick a microphone in her face and say, "Hey, Marilyn, I hear blondes have more fun! I'm sure our viewers are wondering if that's *true!*" The kids would've broken up at that.

He was thinking so hard about what he *should* have said, he almost missed Cinnamon's introduction.

"Cinnamon has two sisters, Jenny and Megan,"

said her partner, a dark-haired girl named Carrie. "She'd be Jackie Onassis from history. Last year, Cinnamon went to Ireland with her parents, and she kissed the Blarney Stone."

Jerry couldn't help envying the Blarney Stone just a tiny bit.

"And once on a dare," Carrie said, reading Cinnamon's paper, "she put on the dorkiest clothes she could find and walked the whole length of the mall!"

"I could've died, I looked so bad!" Cinnamon said, giggling.

Jerry was glad he'd chosen his clothes carefully today.

The other groups were finishing, and Ms. Robertson told everyone to return to their seats.

Jerry moved back to his desk. Brenda plopped into her chair and turned to him.

"That offer of help still stands," she whispered. "And don't say you don't need help getting cool. No offense, but everything about you screams *dork*."

There was no point arguing with her or pretending it wasn't true. He'd just proved it for everyone to see.

"I know how you feel." She leaned closer and whispered so softly, he could barely hear her. "It takes one to know one."

# Chapter Three

Social studies had just begun when the intercom speaker clicked on.

"Ms. Robertson?" It was a woman's voice.

"Yes?" Ms. Robertson called.

"Is Jerry Flack in your class?"

Ms. Robertson's eyelashes fluttered, and she turned to him. "Yes, he is."

"Would you send him to the office, please?"

"Sure." She spoke more softly now. "Go ahead, Jerry. Come back as soon as you can."

Jerry felt everyone's eyes on him as he got up and walked self-consciously across the front of the room and out the door. He knew what this was about, of course. Mrs. Barnaby had said that Mr. Meyer might call him to the office about the vandalism in his homeroom. His heart ka-blammed into his ribcage, and he realized fleetingly that his armpits were wet.

The last time Jerry had been sent to the principal's office, he was in first grade. His teacher had been so impressed with Jerry, she had sent him to read to the principal. Mr. Hovet had smiled while Jerry read him the story from the third-grade reading book. He patted Jerry's shoulder and told him he'd done an excellent job.

Jerry had found out later that his teacher thought he should be moved up to second grade. His parents had decided, though, after talking with a child development specialist, to leave him with children his age.

This time, Jerry wouldn't be getting compliments from the principal. He'd have to answer questions about finding his homeroom wrecked. He wondered if Mr. Meyer suspected that he and Craig had done it.

How could he have been so stupid as to let Craig talk him into helping him mess up the classroom?

He pulled open the heavy door to the main office and approached the counter on shaky legs. Two women, one with gray hair, one with blond hair, sat at desks on either side of the room.

"Yes?" said the gray-haired woman. A chrome nameplate sat on her desk. It said MRS. BRUIN.

"I'm Jerry Flack. I was—"

"Oh, yes. Have a seat. We're waiting for another student."

Jerry sat in a plastic chair next to the wall. The door opened and Craig walked in. He grinned at Jerry and leaned over. "We don't know nothin'."

Jerry looked at the floor and didn't respond.

"You boys may go in to see Mr. Meyer now," said Mrs. Bruin from her desk.

Mr. Meyer's name was stenciled on a plaque above his door. Below that, it said ASSISTANT PRINCIPAL.

Jerry followed Craig into Mr. Meyer's office.

"Sit down, boys."

Mr. Meyer sat behind his desk, a huge man who looked as if he could bench-press a Buick or two. The shiny substance on his hair reminded Jerry of the polyurethane that had been applied to the wooden floor of his room in the old house a few years ago. Mr. Meyer had apparently chosen the high-gloss finish; it reflected the light from the ceiling fixture overhead.

Mr. Meyer didn't look happy.

"Which one of you is Craig?"

"Me," Craig said.

Mr. Meyer gazed out from under furry eyebrows. "And you're Jerry Flack?" Jerry nodded. "I understand there was some vandalism in your classroom this morning."

"That's right, Mr. Meyer." Craig nodded and

leaned forward in his seat. "It was really a mess."

"Did either of you see anyone in or around the classroom as you came toward it?"

"Nope," Craig said. "Nobody."

"How about you, Jerry? Did you see anyone?"

"I didn't see anyone come out of the room," Jerry said, looking at Mr. Meyer's desk.

"I understand that the students had been gone only five minutes or so before the damage occurred," Mr. Meyer said.

"That's about right," Craig said. He turned to Jerry. "Wouldn't you say about five minutes?"

"Uh, yes."

"It's strange, don't you think," Mr. Meyer said, "that someone who wasn't a student in that homeroom would run into the classroom and do all that damage and run out again? And not be seen?"

"Very strange," said Craig, nodding. "He was very fast. Or she. It could have been a girl."

Craig was obviously having fun with Mr. Meyer. Jerry wished that Craig would just shut up.

"At Hawthorne Middle School, we consider vandalism a very serious matter," said Mr. Meyer. "When we catch a vandal, we're rough."

Craig nodded again.

"And this is particularly galling because this occurred on the first day of school," Mr. Meyer said. "The first *hour* of the day, the first few *minutes* of the school year.

"Craig," he went on, "I understand that you were suspended twice at Hemingway Elementary."

Craig, still looking as innocent as a newborn, nodded.

"I know Bob Brown, the principal down at Hemingway," Mr. Meyer said, leaning back in his seat. "He doesn't suspend students for minor infractions."

Mr. Meyer turned to Jerry. "I don't know much about you. You're new in town, right?"

"Yes."

Now Mr. Meyer leaned forward over his desk. "I want you boys to know that I'm going to keep my eye on you both. You even sneeze, I'm going to find out about it. You got that?"

"Yes," Craig said, nodding.

"How about you, Flack? You understand what I'm saying?"

"Yes."

"I'll be watching. And I'm warning you: One false move from either of you, and I'll kick your butts out the door. You got that?"

"Yes," both boys said together.

"Remember that. Now get out of here."

Craig jumped up from his chair and smiled at Mr. Meyer. "See you, Mr. Meyer," he said.

"I hope not."

Jerry got up and walked out of Mr. Meyer's office, through the main office, and into the hall.

Craig followed him. Once in the hall, he snorted. "He thinks he's so tough!" He lowered his voice and mimicked Mr. Meyer. "'I'll kick your butts out the door.'"

Jerry, who had never hit anyone other than his sister, had to restrain himself from slugging Craig in the mouth. He turned and headed down the hall.

"Hey, where are you going, Flack?"

"Where do you think?" Jerry growled, hurrying away. "Back to class."

Craig laughed and called out, "Okay. Hey, we were really cool in there, weren't we?"

Jerry didn't bother to answer.

"Why were you called to the office?" Brenda asked Jerry after third-period math class. It was the second time she'd asked him. The first time, he'd changed the subject.

"Someone messed up my homeroom," Jerry said. "Mr. Meyer wanted to know if I'd seen anyone coming out of the room."

"Oh." Brenda seemed satisfied. "Hey, you want to have lunch together? We'll talk more about your Cool lessons."

Jerry had to admit that his efforts so far had been disastrous. He had succeeded only in getting himself in trouble with Mr. Meyer and making himself look foolish in front of Cinnamon.

Besides, Brenda seemed awfully smart. Maybe

she could help. What did he have to lose?

He shrugged. "Okay." Then he added, "But don't you think this is like the blind leading the blind?"

"Good point," Brenda said. "But remember, a great football coach doesn't have to be a great full-back."

"I see what you mean," Jerry said.

"I just did something that a cool guy would do," Brenda said.

"What's that?"

"I used a football metaphor. Cool guys talk about sports whenever they can. Even to make a point about something else."

"I'll keep that in mind," Jerry said.

Jerry and Brenda walked into the cafeteria.

"Oh, there are two of my friends," Brenda said. "Come on; we'll sit with them." Jerry followed Brenda to a table at the side of the room.

Two girls sat across the table from each other. One was the mirror image of the other. They both had frizzy brown hair that grew wild around their faces like the manes on a couple of lions.

"Hi, Brenda. Sit down," one of the girls said. "We were waiting for you. We want to fill this table with nice people."

"Yeah, no snobs," said the other girl.

"Guys, this is Jerry Flack," Brenda said. "Jerry, this is Kim and Kat Henley."

"Hi," they said in unison.

"I'm the oldest," Kim said.

Kat rolled her eyes. "She always says that. But only by ten minutes."

"It doesn't matter by how much," Kim said. "The fact is, I'm the older sister."

"She's the one with the mole on her cheek," Kat said. "See?"

Now Kim rolled her eyes. "It's not a mole, it's a beauty mark," she said. "All the supermodels have them."

"It looks exactly like the one on my foot," Kat said. "The doctor said it was a mole."

Brenda jumped in. "Let's get some food."

They left their books and notebooks at the table and headed for the end of the line at the side of the cafeteria.

Brenda said in Jerry's ear, "Kim and Kat are two of the smartest kids in the whole sixth grade."

"Really?" Jerry asked.

"They seem dumb when they're together because they're always arguing about something stupid."

They walked along the line. The cafeteria workers, all women with gray hair tucked into hairnets, handed them plates of sloppy joes, green beans, fruit cocktail, and cookies.

They made their way back to the table and sat down. Brenda nudged Jerry. "Look who just made an entrance."

He turned to look. "Gabe Marshall," Jerry murmured.

Gabe was fuzzy, but Jerry could pick out his red Adidas shirt. Jerry was pretty sure he was walking with the guy who had been rollerblading with him that morning. They strolled over to a table at the back and left their backpacks before heading for a second line on the other side of the cafeteria.

"Look at his hair," Brenda marveled. "Any girl would kill for that hair."

"An accident in the gene pool," Jerry said.

"Of course, it could be chemically curled," Kim said. "I read that more guys are getting perms these days."

"He doesn't look like the perm type," Kat said, staring across the room at Gabe. "Can you see him sitting in a salon chair under a hair dryer, surrounded by women in curlers?"

Jerry had to laugh. He couldn't picture it.

Jerry saw Cinnamon then, sitting at a table not far from him. She'd already gotten her lunch and, along with three other girls at her table, she was watching Gabe.

Brenda followed Jerry's gaze. "Don't worry," she said. "We'll get you so cool, Cinnamon will be begging you for your phone number."

That was something else Jerry couldn't picture, but he liked the way it sounded. He liked it a lot.

# Chapter Four

"Cool."

Jerry sprawled on his bed with his dog, Sarsaparilla, and stared at the page in his science magazine. Minutes before, he had been studying the most recent issue of *Ultimate Cool* that he'd picked up at the drugstore. He had gotten bored, however, and replaced it with his favorite magazine, *The Amazing World of Science*.

"Learn about Newton's second law," it said on the top of page 23. "Build a hovercraft and learn what factors affect the motion of an object."

"I could do that," Jerry murmured, stroking Sarsaparilla's nose. Sassy, which they called her for short, was a curious mix of terrier and spaniel. She lay with her head on her paws, her tail thumping the bed, ready as usual to spring into action if the situation called for it. Sassy was always eager for mischief.

Jerry studied the picture of the hovercraft. "That would be an awesome project, probably the kind of thing Stephen Hawking did when he was a kid."

The famous physicist stared down at Jerry from the poster on his wall. Next to Hawking was a poster of Albert Einstein. These were Jerry's heroes.

His bedroom door burst open, and six-year-old Melissa charged in, giggling, and threw herself on the bed. She was followed by her new friend Rachel, who stood quietly just inside the door.

"Show us a trick," Melissa said.

"I'm busy now," Jerry said.

"We're bored," Melissa said. "And Mom's on the warpath. The paper carrier threw the paper in the bushes again, and it took Mom half an hour to find it. Hey, how come you're not wearing your glasses?"

"I'm trying to get used to not wearing them."

"Can you see without your glasses?"

"Not very well."

"How come you want to get used to not seeing?"

"Leave me alone."

Melissa scrambled off the bed and ran to the far wall.

"How many digits?" she said, holding up four fingers.

"What?" Jerry was still reading.

"How many digits am I holding up?"

Jerry didn't look up. "Two."

"You didn't even look."

"Go away, Melissa."

"Not until you show us a trick. I promised Rachel you would."

Jerry put the magazine down and sighed. "Okay." He'd been working on a science trick anyway, and he wanted to see if he could pull it off. "First get me the bucket from the basement and a pitcher of water."

"Come on, Rach!" Melissa squealed. The girls ran out of the room.

Jerry went over to the cardboard box where he kept all the materials he needed for his science tricks. He pulled a plastic cup out of it, then went to his desk, picked up an index card, and slid it into his pocket.

When the girls returned, Jerry said, "Put the bucket on the floor here, Melissa. Okay, now you guys sit on the bed and watch carefully.

"I've been working on increasing the power of my mind," Jerry said dramatically. "I'm going to make the water in this cup do exactly as I say. The pitcher of water, please."

Melissa giggled and handed him the pitcher. Jerry held up the plastic cup and poured it full to the brim.

"An ordinary index card," he said, pulling the white rectangle from his pocket and holding it up.

He placed the card over the rim of the cup. Then slowly, holding the card in place, he turned the cup upside down.

*"I order you, water, to stay inside the cup!"*

Jerry carefully let go of the index card. The water stayed inside the cup. Melissa and Rachel gasped and clapped.

After a few more seconds, Jerry said, *"I order you, water—out of the cup NOW!"*

The water splashed out of the cup, along with the index card, into the bucket.

"Wow, Jerry!" Melissa squealed. "How'd you *do* that?"

"I told you," Jerry said, shrugging. "I've been working on the power of my mind. It's a very powerful thing, you know."

"Amazing," Rachel whispered.

"It's a trick, Rach," Melissa said. "Don't be too impressed. He never tells how he does it. But it was fun, Jerry. Come on, Rach."

Melissa skipped out of the room with Rachel close behind.

Jerry smiled. The trick had worked perfectly. He'd drilled a tiny hole in the plastic cup yesterday when he first read about this trick. With his finger over the hole, the water didn't fall because the air pressure pushing up on the card was a greater force than the gravity pulling down on it. When he wanted the water to splash out of the cup, all he had to do was take his finger off the hole. That let in air, and the air pressure was the same inside and outside the cup. Gravity took over and pulled the water into the bucket.

His mother appeared at the door. "Jerry, there's a phone call for you."

"You're kidding," Jerry said. His stomach fluttered a little.

"No, I'm not kidding," his mother said. "And after you hang up, let me know. I need to call our paper carrier."

"Okay," Jerry said, distracted. He couldn't figure out who would be calling him.

He hurried into his parents' room and picked up the receiver.

"Hello?"

"Flack? Brenda McAdams." She sounded excited, and Jerry was immediately curious.

"Hi," he said.

"Listen," she said, "I was just watching TV, and there was this woman who rips jeans for the stars."

"She rips jeans?"

"You've seen famous people on TV wearing jeans with tears and frayed hems?"

"Yeah."

"Well, a professional jeans distresser probably worked on the jeans to make them look that way."

"You're kidding."

"No, I'm not," Brenda said. "Anyway, this woman gave some tips on how to make jeans look lived-in. If you want to, we could get together, and I could help you rip your jeans in the coolest places and make them look worn out."

"That sounds good," Jerry said. "Would tomorrow after school be okay?"

"Yes indeedy. See you." Brenda hung up.

Jerry shook his head. He was amazed at how many details went into being cool. He had a suspicion that despite all his research, he was just beginning to scratch the surface of coolness.

Everyone was seated when the bell rang signaling the beginning of language arts class.

Everyone, that is, except Gabe. He loped through the door a few seconds late and headed for the back of the room.

"Gabe," Ms. Robertson said, "you should be in your seat by the time the bell rings."

Gabe grinned. "I was in the bathroom."

The girls giggled and the guys smirked.

Ms. Robertson said, "We're going to start the year reading short stories. Do any of you enjoy reading stories outside of school?"

Jerry made a move to raise his hand, but he realized what he was doing and put his hand back on his desk.

Five students raised their hands.

"Do you have a favorite author, Brenda?" Ms. Robertson asked.

"Ray Bradbury's my favorite short story writer," Brenda said. "I love 'The Man Upstairs,' and 'The Dwarf.'"

"Those are excellent stories," Ms. Robertson agreed. "Bradbury's use of language is exquisite."

Jerry glanced back and thought he saw Robin roll her eyes at Cinnamon. Bradbury was Jerry's favorite short story author, too, but he kept his mouth shut.

"I like short stories," Gabe said. "The shorter the better. And ones with lots of pictures. Hey, how come books we read don't have pictures anymore?"

There were giggles from some of the girls.

"What a dope," Brenda murmured. She was facing forward, so only Jerry heard her.

"Books without pictures are still filled with imagery," Ms. Robertson said. "A skillful author will use words to create pictures in your head."

Gabe covered his head with his hands. "That sounds painful," he said. The class cracked up.

Ms. Robertson was not amused. "Gabe, if you have a comment, please raise your hand."

He raised his hand.

"Yes?" she asked.

"That sounds painful."

Some of the kids roared with laughter. Jerry was

starting to feel sorry for Ms. Robertson.

"Gabe," Ms. Robertson said, "in the future, I hope your remarks add something worthwhile to the class discussion. You're not in elementary school anymore, are you?"

Gabe raised his hand.

"Yes?" she said. There was an edge to her voice.

"No, I'm not in elementary school anymore," he said.

More kids laughed. They seemed awed that Gabe would keep it up like that.

Ms. Robertson frowned and wrote Gabe's name on the board. "Your behavior, Gabe, forces me to start using my check policy. One more smart remark, and I'll put a check after your name. That earns you a detention after school."

Gabe continued to grin, and he shrugged. But he stayed quiet through the rest of language arts and social studies classes. He didn't need to push it. His status had risen with just those few wisecracks.

After social studies, Gabe strutted out of the classroom, surrounded by half a dozen admirers. Cinnamon walked along next to him, looking up at his face, beaming.

Brenda appeared at Jerry's side. "Can you believe it? The guy's almost brain-dead, and look at the attention he gets."

"You've got to admit, though, Gabe's cool," Jerry said. "And funny."

"I think he's a jerk. A gorgeous, idiotic jerk."

"You think he's gorgeous?"

"Sure. But then he opens his mouth and ruins everything."

"Yeah," Jerry said. But he was thinking. Maybe he could think of some funny things to say in class, too. Ms. Robertson wouldn't like it, but maybe it would get Cinnamon to notice him.

He'd have to think about it.

# Chapter Five

As Jerry walked out of the cafeteria, someone threw an arm around his shoulder.

"Hey, Jerry, whaddaya say?"

It was Craig Fox.

"Oh, hi," Jerry said. He wished Craig would go away. In fact, he never wanted to see Craig again for as long as he lived. That would be impossible, of course, because Craig was his locker partner.

Craig turned around and said, "Hey, guys, this is Jerry Flack, the guy I told you about."

Jerry turned to see who Craig was talking to and nearly choked. It was Gabe Marshall himself.

Gabe nodded to him.

"Jerry's cool," Craig said.

Gabe grinned. "Fox's been talking about how you guys started the school year off with a bang."

Jerry tried to smile. "Oh, yeah."

This was amazing. All the kids in Jerry's old school had called him a dork. It was a unanimous opinion. Once, at the end of fifth grade, Jerry had been standing in the hall with his best friend, Drew Hepner, and two other guys that Jerry hung around with. The most popular girl in school walked by with three of her friends. She pointed to Jerry and the others and called out, "Oh, look. It must be a dork convention!" Her friends shrieked with laughter.

It was the ultimate humiliation.

Jerry knew that his family was moving, and it was at that moment he decided he was going to change his image. He wasn't going through another horrible year as one of the dorks.

And now here he was—just four short months later—walking down the hall of his new school with Gabe, the coolest guy in his class. And Craig had just described *Jerry* as cool. If only the kids at his old school could see him now.

Craig pointed to another boy who stood with them. He was the kid Jerry had seen Gabe with several times. "This is Tony."

"Hi," Jerry said.

"How're you doin'?" Tony murmured.

"Great."

"You rollerblade, Flack?" Gabe asked.

"Who, me?" Jerry asked. "Uh, sure. I rollerblade all the time. Rollerblading's my favorite thing to do."

"We'll go some time," Gabe said.

"Great."

"See you, Flack," Craig said.

"I'll touch base with you guys later," Jerry said.

He was proud that he'd pulled that baseball metaphor out of thin air.

The guys made a right turn and kept walking down the hall.

Jerry, stunned at the attention, kept walking and climbed the stairs. There was a tap on his shoulder.

"Hi," Brenda said. She walked along beside him. "I saw you walking with Gabe and company. Pretty impressive."

"Yeah! I used a baseball metaphor. And they invited me to go rollerblading sometime."

"Do you know how?"

"Well, I'm not very good."

"Have you ever been on skates during this life-time?"

"Not exactly."

"That's what I thought," she said. "What are you going to do when Gabe wants to go rollerblading?"

"I don't know. Maybe I'll learn how to skate." He turned to Brenda. "Didn't you say you went to

Hemingway Elementary?" Brenda nodded. "Do you know Craig Fox?"

"Yeah," she said. "He was on the edge of the popular crowd at Hemingway and works hard at being cool. He's also a jerk. One time in fourth grade he pushed a first grader into a locker and closed the door. It locked, and our teacher had to call the janitor to get him out. Meanwhile, the kid was screaming his head off. Craig was suspended for a week, and he had to go visit the school counselor twice a week for the rest of the semester. He thought it was pretty funny."

"Looks like he's buddies with Gabe and Tony," Jerry said.

Brenda nodded. "I think Gabe and Craig live across the street from each other. They've been friends for a long time."

"That explains it."

"Well, Flack, I hope for your sake that they never ask you to go rollerblading," Brenda said, turning away. "I've got to stop at my locker first, but I'll see you in science class."

"Yeah, see you."

Jerry knew Brenda was right. He shouldn't have lied to those guys about being able to rollerblade. But if he'd told them the truth, they would have thought he was a dork.

It was obvious to him already that pulling off this

Cool Guy thing was going to be tricky. He wanted to hang out with Gabe and his friends, but he wanted to stay away from Craig.

If he could convince Gabe and Cinnamon for even a couple of weeks that he was really cool, it would be the best couple of weeks of his life.

He started to whistle and headed down the hall, but he realized what he was doing and closed his mouth. Cool Guys probably didn't whistle on their way to class.

Jerry stood next to a counter that ran under the rows of windows in his science class. The minute he'd walked in the day before, he'd known that this would be his favorite class. The whole room was filled with fascinating stuff.

Hanging on the far wall was a huge Periodic Table of the Elements. He knew what it was, even though he couldn't see it well enough to make out the individual elements listed. He didn't have to see them, though. He knew the chart by heart, all the elements and their symbols.

Under the chart was a sink, and next to that was an aquarium filled with guppies and angelfish and neon tetras. Jerry walked along the counter, marveling at everything he saw. There were books about weather and rocks and minerals and plants. There was a bank of computers along another wall, a TV monitor overhead, a CD laser scanner, microscopes and magnifying glasses, a Bunsen burner, test tubes and petri dishes. A robin's nest sat on one shelf, and a Baltimore oriole's nest sat on another. A hornet's nest hung from the ceiling in one corner, and a tiny hummingbird's nest sat on a shelf next to the teacher's desk.

To Jerry, this room was better than Disney World, Great America, and Oceans of Fun all rolled into one.

He was glad Cinnamon wasn't in this class, or Gabe, or Robin. He thought he spotted a familiar face and squinted to see better.

Yup, Tony was in his class. He'd have to be careful in here, or Tony might tell Gabe that Jerry was a science nerd.

A blurry Brenda walked into the room and waved at him. She said hi to a half-dozen kids as she made her way to her seat. She sat with Kim Henley on one side and Kat Henley on the other. Jerry couldn't see well enough to make out which one was which.

Mr. Hooten talked about the things they would study this year: plants, animals, rocks and minerals. It all sounded interesting, but when Mr. Hooten suggested that students could earn extra credit by doing projects on their own and keeping a science journal, Jerry leaned forward to hear every word. He was already doing those things! Now he could talk to a real scientist, Mr. Hooten, about his experiments, and get extra credit, too. Not that he'd need the extra credit in science. It was his best subject.

"This is going to be a fun class," Brenda said after the period ended. The Henley sisters and two others, a blond girl and a dark-haired kid, stood next to her. "Hey, have you met Chad Newsome?" Brenda asked. "And this is Aubrey Lane." The blonde bobbed her head at Jerry. "Guys, this is Jerry Flack."

"Hi," they all said.

"The five of us hung out a lot this summer," Brenda said, grinning. "I guess the last time I saw these guys all together was at Sal's Pizza. The twins are *maniacs* over triple cheese."

Kim, the one with the mole/beauty mark, rolled her eyes. "Don't call us 'the twins,'" she said.

"We're individuals," said Kat.

"Don't even call us the Henley sisters," said Kim.

"Call us by our names," said Kat.

"Sorry," Brenda said. "I forgot."

"Remember"—Kim turned to Jerry—"I'm Kim. I have the beauty mark."

"It's really a mole," Kat said, "but if you insist—"

"I have to stop at my locker," Jerry interrupted, not wanting to hear the argument again.

"See you in computer class," Kim and Kat said in unison.

"Yeah, see you," Chad said. "I'm in your class, too."

"Me, too. In fact, I'm in most of your classes," Aubrey said with a smile.

Jerry had thought these two were in more than just his science class, but because most faces were pretty blurry, he hadn't been sure.

"Bye," Brenda called out.

Jerry hurried to his locker at the end of the hall. He worked the combination lock and opened it. He stared at what he saw.

It was only the second day of school, and already the locker was a mess. Craig had thrown his books into it so they stood sideways or upside down. One was partly open with a dirty running shoe crammed inside, creasing some of the soiled pages. The mess took over the entire locker.

No wonder Craig hadn't cared which shelf was his. It didn't matter; he used both of them.

Jerry cleared off the top shelf and pushed Craig's stuff onto the second shelf. Then he organized the top shelf with books from his morning classes. He took a second look at it. It didn't look like the shelf of a cool guy. He ripped out a blank piece of notebook paper, crumpled it, and jammed it into a space on the shelf. That was more like it; it looked messier now.

That would have to do for the time being. Later he could figure out other ways to mess up his shelf but still keep it reasonably organized.

He shut the locker and headed to computer

class feeling pretty good. His disguise was working well today. After all, the Cool Guys had asked him to go rollerblading.

As long as he didn't have to actually *skate*, things just might work out.

# Chapter Six

"The professional jeans ripper said one of the coolest places for a rip is just above the knee."

Brenda sat cross-legged on the floor in Jerry's room, staring at his pant leg. Sassy sat next to her.

"Let's mark it right here," she said. She drew a line with a fine-point marker above Jerry's left knee. "And let's rip the other leg, too." She marked it. "Another place for a rip—and the woman said this is really sexy—is on the thigh, just below the pocket."

Jerry wasn't sure he wanted to be *sexy*. Right now, cool was what he was aiming for.

"Let's start with the rips above the knees," he said.

"Okay," Brenda said. "Go take 'em off. I'm going to start the rip with a seam ripper."

Jerry went into the bathroom, changed out of his jeans into a different pair, returned, and handed the jeans to Brenda.

"Okay." She opened an inch-long slit in the fabric with the sharp instrument. She grinned at Jerry. "Ready to let 'er rip?"

"Rip away!" Jerry said. "Then I get to do the next one."

Brenda dug her fingers into the fabric and pulled. The fabric made a soft ripping sound.

Brenda held up the jeans. "What do you think?"

"That's the coolest rip I've ever seen," Jerry answered, nodding, with a big grin on his face. Brenda laughed.

"Let me try one," Jerry said.

"Okay," Brenda said, "but let's not make them symmetrical. We'll put this one right over the knee."

Jerry used the seam ripper to start it.

"Ready?" he called out and yanked on the fabric. "Let 'er *r-r-rip!*" He held it up. "How'd I do?"

Brenda beamed. "An excellent rip if I ever saw one."

"Yeah, but is it *cool?*"

"This," she said dramatically, taking the jeans from him, "is the ultimate in cool rips. I congratulate you on your work of art." She grinned at him.

Jerry gazed at Brenda. She had a nice smile. It was good to be away from school and all the pressure to act cool.

"Thanks," he said, grinning back.

"I'll pull out some of the threads around the rips so they look natural," Brenda said. "Now we should fray the jeans at the hem."

"How do we do that?"

"Got any coarse sandpaper?"

"I think so, in the garage. I'll get it."

Sassy trotted with Jerry out to the garage and back. When they returned to his room, Jerry found Brenda looking through his science magazine.

"This is great," she said.

"Yeah," Jerry said. "I'm going to build the hovercraft on page twenty-three."

Brenda turned several pages. "It lifts you off the floor?"

"With just a vacuum cleaner motor. I'm going to get the motor after school tomorrow."

"Cool."

"Here's the sandpaper." Jerry handed it to her.

Brenda put down the magazine and began sanding away at the hem of one leg. "You work on the other leg. When we're done, we'll bleach the jeans."

Jerry sat on the floor next to her and worked.

Brenda sanded a few minutes before she spoke again. "I realized something this morning about Gabe and the other guys," she said. "You ever notice how they move? They don't just walk, they strut."

Jerry looked up at her. "I hadn't really thought about it, but you're right."

Brenda went on. "Gabe's head bobs a little and there's some shoulder movement. It's a lot like a jock walk, only cockier. He walks like he has huge biceps, with his arms swinging away from his body, so he won't get chafed."

"Gabe doesn't have big biceps," Jerry said.

"Exactly," Brenda said. "He's such a phony. Why don't you try it?"

"You mean, now?"

"Sure."

Jerry stood up feeling self-conscious. "Maybe I should practice first."

"Come on, you can do it," Brenda said. "Walk in the door and make an entrance."

Jerry walked normally out of the room, followed by Sassy. He squinted at himself in the mirror at the end of the hall and took three practice steps while Sassy watched calmly. Jerry's reflection was blurry, but he was sure his walk didn't look cool.

"I don't think I'm ready to try it yet," he said.

"I promise not to laugh," Brenda called out from his room. "I'll give you a critique."

He took a deep breath. "Okay."

Jerry bobbed his head, and walked into the room, swinging his shoulders and arms. Sassy trotted along next to him.

Brenda watched him, frowning. "You're not strutting, you're parading."

"Okay, then you do it," Jerry said.

Brenda got up. "I don't know if I can." She grimaced, concentrating hard, took a big breath, then walked across the room with the best swaggering strut Jerry had ever seen.

"Man, you're good!" he said.

"Really?"

"Yeah. Do it again. I'll analyze your movements."

She did.

"You lead with your shoulders," Jerry said. "And your arms swing away from your body, kind of like a gorilla."

Brenda grinned. "So as not to get chafed from my swinging biceps. Now you try."

"No, I'll practice on my own later."

"We should schedule a Strut Watch before school tomorrow," Brenda said, settling down next to him on the floor. "Every guy has his own style. Maybe you can pick up some pointers by observing a bunch of guys when they don't know they're being watched."

"Good idea."

"I'll meet you at 7:40 next to the big oak. The Cool Guys do a lot of strutting around that tree." She grinned. "That's where I first saw you."

Jerry gazed at Brenda and that smile again. Her

eyes crinkled a little at the edges, giving her a mischievous, fun look.

"Okay," he said, smiling back. "Seven-forty. I'll be there."

The next morning, Jerry pulled on his new, torn jeans and looked in the mirror. He squinted. He grabbed his glasses off the bureau, put them on, and gazed into the mirror again.

The jeans looked like something a rock star would wear, faded and torn, with a couple of loose threads hanging from the rips above the knees. The hems were worn and frayed.

Brenda had done an excellent job. The jeans were, in a word, *cool*. Remarkably so.

Next, Jerry pulled on a Hard Rock Café T-shirt that his aunt had brought him from New York. His costume was complete.

He tossed his glasses back onto the bureau, picked up his backpack, and headed downstairs for breakfast.

"Hi, Mom. Hi, Dad. Hi, Squirt." He loped to the kitchen cabinet and pulled out a box of Cheerios.

"Tell Jerry not to call me Squirt," Melissa said. She leaned over her cereal bowl, milk running down her chin.

"It's a sign of affection," Jerry's mom told her.

"No it's not," Jerry said.

Mrs. Flack looked up at Jerry and did a double

take. "Where did you get those jeans?"

Mr. Flack looked up from the *Time* magazine he was reading and stared at Jerry's knees, his eyes wide.

"I got 'em from you," Jerry said to his mom. "Last week." He poured the cereal into a bowl.

"They're ruined!"

"Brenda and I worked on them. Now they have character."

"They have air vents," Jerry's dad observed. "Comfortable in the warm weather but a bit chilly come winter."

"But think of the money I spent!" Mrs. Flack said. She walked around Jerry, examining his jeans from different angles. "Thirty-two dollars for new jeans, and now they look ready to throw away."

"Could you iron on patches?" Mr. Flack asked.

Jerry gawked at his dad. "You're kidding, right?"

Geez, he thought. No wonder he was a dork; it was hereditary. Iron-on knee patches would brand him for eternity the Biggest Dork in the Universe.

His dad shrugged.

"He's kidding; I know he's kidding," Jerry mumbled to reassure himself. He turned to his mom. "I could use a couple more pairs." He went to the refrigerator for milk. "Buy the stone-washed kind. It'll save us some work."

"No way, Jerry," his mother said. "I'm not buying brand-new jeans so you can ruin them!" She ran a hand through her hair, exasperated. Then she gazed at him keenly. "Why aren't you wearing your glasses?"

"I don't need them."

"He does too," Melissa said. "He couldn't even see the digits I held up yesterday." She held up three fingers. "How many?"

Jerry ignored her. "I have to go to school a little early. I'm meeting Brenda."

"Can you see the blackboard at school?" Mrs. Flack asked.

"Sure."

"Just not what's written on it," Melissa said.

"I want to see those glasses on your face when you leave this morning," Mrs. Flack said.

Jerry shrugged. "Okay." He knew if he only wore them from the front door until he was a block away, he wouldn't have dents on his nose. And his mom would be satisfied.

No problem. Everything was cool.

Brenda nudged Jerry. "Here comes the master strutter."

They leaned against the tall oak and watched Gabe, followed by Tony, wind his way around the clusters of kids who waited outside the school. Once again, heads turned as they moved through the crowd.

"Gabe's walk is like yours was last night," Jerry said.

Brenda grinned. "Thanks. You're right, he leads with his head, like a rooster. Tony's strut is different, though. See? His head bobs, but look how he holds his hands, bent forward at the wrists and swinging ahead of him."

"Hey, Flack." Craig stepped in front of Jerry.

"Hi, Fox," Jerry said.

"We're all playing street hockey after school at Gabe's house. You want to come?"

"Uh—" Jerry faltered. What should he say? He couldn't say he was going to go buy a vacuum cleaner motor for a science project. That was too dorky. And he certainly couldn't admit that he didn't know how to skate after lying about it yesterday. "I have to go buy a new pair of skates. Mine are worn out."

"Cool. What kind are you getting?"

"Um, I'm not sure yet." Jerry didn't look at Brenda, but he wished she wasn't here. He felt self-conscious telling lies in front of her.

"You getting them for stunts or hockey?"

Gabe and Tony suddenly appeared at Craig's side with Cinnamon and Robin. "I haven't decided yet," Jerry said. "I do both."

Jerry suddenly felt very warm, and his face tingled.

Craig laughed. "I can't wait to see you skate, man. You must be awesome."

"I've been told that," Jerry said, forcing a smile.

Sweat bloomed under his arms. Geez, the lies

60

were really piling up. He'd told four lies in just the last few seconds.

Cinnamon looked at Jerry with interest. He was glad he was wearing his cool ripped jeans. Maybe she'd look at his clothes and not notice that he was starting to get the shakes.

"You playing street hockey with us, Flack?" Gabe asked.

"Sorry, I've been sidelined for a while," Jerry said, hoping they noticed his sports metaphor. "Maybe some other time."

"How about tomorrow?" Gabe asked. He leveled his gaze at Jerry.

Jerry flinched under Gabe's stare. "Uh, I'll have to see."

"You name the time," Gabe said. "We'll be there."

"Okay," Jerry said, looking away. "I'll have to check my calendar."

"You do that." Gabe turned and swaggered away with his admiring fans following him.

Brenda stepped close to Jerry and asked in a low voice, "Did you get the feeling Gabe knows you're lying?"

"Yeah," Jerry said. He let out a breath he didn't know he'd been holding.

"Me too. What are you going to do?"

"I don't know," Jerry said. "I was going to buy the vacuum cleaner motor after school for my science project. But maybe I should buy skates instead."

"Is that what you want?"

"No, I want to build that hovercraft. But maybe if I learned how to rollerblade—"

"It would take you months of constant practice to get good enough to play street hockey with those guys," Brenda said.

"Yeah, I guess you're right."

He didn't *want* to learn how to rollerblade. He wanted to build that cool hovercraft. Besides, a guy could get killed on rollerblades.

He looked at Brenda, and she returned his gaze sympathetically.

It seemed as if the lies he'd been spinning lately were getting tangled around his feet. They hadn't succeeded in tripping him yet, but he'd have to watch his step very, very carefully.

"We're going to begin with the elements of stories," Ms. Robertson said. "Who can tell me what the *setting* is?"

"It's what I'm doing now," Gabe called out. "Setting at my desk."

The class broke up.

Jerry saw the opportunity for comedy and grabbed it. "Just like setting hens. Careful, Gabe. You don't want broken eggs on your pants." He looked at Ms. Robertson. "Excuse me, that was a fowl yolk."

Brenda, Aubrey, and Chad and a few others

burst out laughing. Ms. Robertson laughed, too. The rest of the room was silent. Carrie, who sat across the aisle from him, sighed loudly and rolled her eyes.

"You're quite a punster, Jerry," Ms. Robertson said.

The heat rose in Jerry's face. Wasn't his comment funny? He slid down a few inches in his chair.

"Jerry," said Ms. Robertson, "will you please tell the class what the setting of a story really is?"

She looked at him expectantly. Jerry knew the answer, but saying it would just make everything worse.

"I don't know," he mumbled.

A dark-haired girl raised her hand. "It's when and where the story takes place."

"That's right," Ms. Robertson said. "The setting is an important element of stories and novels. Just think about *The Wizard of Oz* and how the story begins on a little farm in Kansas. It's quite a contrast to the magical Land of Oz that Dorothy dreams about."

"I liked all the little people in the movie," Robin said.

"The Wicked Witch of the West is my personal favorite," Gabe said sarcastically.

The girls laughed.

"And that brings us to characterization," said Ms. Robertson. "What would *The Wizard of Oz* be without all of those wonderful characters? Innocent Dorothy; the evil witch; the wizard, who wasn't really a wizard at all—"

"He wasn't a wizard?" Gabe cried out, pretending dismay. "No one ever told me!"

Loud laughter filled the room.

"Gabe, remember what I said yesterday," Ms. Robertson told him. "I'd like to hear your comments, but only if they contribute."

Jerry turned to Gabe. "She doesn't want any more Flack," he said. "She's got enough of that with me."

The class laughed this time, and so did Ms. Robertson.

"Teacher's pet," Robin murmured loud enough so the whole class heard.

Jerry squinted at Gabe, who glared at him. He turned around and slid down farther in his seat.

How did Gabe always know what was funny and cool and what wasn't? Had he been *born* with coolness running in his veins?

Jerry had the terrible feeling that by the time he learned everything about being cool, the kids would have figured out what he really was.

Just a dork in disguise.

# Chapter Seven

"Okay, think cool," Jerry whispered to himself.

He strutted onto the school grounds. He'd practiced his strut for a whole hour last night. At first, it had been awkward and not the least bit cool. Melissa had even asked him if he had a blister on his foot.

But after the first half hour, he'd gotten the hang of it. The second half hour, he'd perfected it so it looked as if he'd walked that way all his life.

The only problem was that he had to warm up. If he stopped concentrating on his strut for an hour, he had to practice again for two or three minutes to get it just right.

So this morning, he warmed up in the upstairs

hall in front of the mirror. He strutted down the stairs for breakfast, swaggered back up to brush his teeth, then used his new self-confident gait down the sidewalk to school.

He was warmed up now, dressed again in his ripped jeans, and ready to show everyone his stuff.

On the school grounds, he saw Cinnamon standing in a small group, talking to Robin. She glanced over at him and then watched as he strutted across the grass. He could sense her eyes on him, as if her gaze had some tactile effect that he could feel right through his shirt.

He spotted Craig Fox talking with Tony and swaggered over to them.

"Hi," Jerry said to them. He glanced around. Cinnamon had disappeared.

"Hey, Flack," Craig said. "I was just telling Tony that Gabe's *sick* today."

"He is? What's wrong with him?" Too bad Gabe wouldn't see his strut till later.

Craig laughed. "He's not really sick, stupid. He's just not coming to school. He told me yesterday that he was going to fool around at the park. Maybe we should cut out, too."

Tony said, "Yeah." But he didn't seem too enthusiastic.

"If we're going," Craig said, "let's go now before any of the teachers see us. You with us, Flack?"

"Uh, I don't know," Jerry said. He felt the panic

rise in his chest. He wasn't about to play hooky with these guys, but how would he get out of it?

"I figured you'd be the first to cut out, Flack," Craig said, looking disappointed.

Jerry looked up to see a very blurry Ms. Robertson slide up a classroom window on the second floor. He squinted and thought he saw her wave.

He waved back. "Oh, too bad," he said, feeling relief wash over him. "Ms. Robertson just saw me. I guess I'll have to cut some another day."

Craig shrugged. "Okay for you, Flack. I thought you were cool."

"I have her, too," Tony said. "I better stay."

"Okay," Craig said. "I'm gonna go find Gabe." He ran off and disappeared around the side of the school.

Tony turned to Jerry. "Too bad," he said. "It could've been fun. See you, Flack."

Jerry thought it might be his imagination, but Tony seemed a little bit relieved, too. "Yeah, see you," Jerry said.

Brenda appeared suddenly. "Craig and Gabe are such idiots," she said.

Jerry looked at her, surprised. "Did you hear that?"

"Yeah, I was standing right over there. You sure you want to be in with those guys?"

"I don't want to cut school," Jerry said, "or hang

out with Craig, who's a jerk. But I do want to be cool. And I want Cinnamon to notice me."

Brenda rolled her eyes. "Why don't you try something simple?"

"Like what?"

"Like being nice to her. I know it sounds crazy, but it just might work."

"Yeah," Jerry said. "I hadn't thought of that."

"I think you're ready," Brenda said. "I noticed you got the strut down."

Jerry grinned. "I perfected it last night. Cinnamon was watching me a few minutes ago."

"I noticed," Brenda said.

The bell rang and they headed toward the school with the rest of the kids.

"Did you get the motor for the hovercraft last night?" Brenda asked.

"Yeah. It'll work fine. My dad cut the board, too."

"I can't wait to see it in action."

Jerry and Brenda, caught in the middle of the crowd, slowed as the kids funneled through the doors.

Jerry's mind drifted back to what Brenda had said. She was right: He was ready to talk to Cinnamon. He felt a little more confident wearing his ripped jeans and walking with his cool gait.

Maybe he could really get her to notice him by just being nice.

The idea of talking to her made him sweat again, but he decided that it was time to make his move.

Jerry got up and walked into the hall after language arts class. Then he remembered his strut, and it took ten steps before he got warmed up.

"Hey, Jerry, you okay?"

Jerry looked up to see Chad Newsome.

"What do you mean?" Jerry asked.

"You were walking funny," Chad said. "Do you have a stone in your shoe or something?"

"Uh, no," Jerry said. "I'm fine."

Chad looked at him quizzically, but he smiled and moved on.

Jerry spotted Cinnamon ahead in the hall, getting a drink from the fountain. For once, she was alone. His heart began to race, but he remembered what Brenda had said and forced himself to swagger over to her.

He leaned against the wall in a cool pose and watched her drink. She even looked beautiful drinking water. She held her red hair to the side so it wouldn't get wet. She saw him and straightened up.

"Hi," he said.

"Hi." She brushed a drop of water from her lips.

It was only then that he realized he had no idea what he would say to her. She looked at him with her deep blue eyes, waiting for him to speak.

"Is the water good?" he blurted.

She laughed, assuming he was joking. "I'd like soda better."

Jerry laughed, too. "Soda in the water fountain. That's a great idea. Maybe you could patent it."

Cinnamon laughed and looked at him with interest. "I hear you're great on rollerblades."

"Oh, I wouldn't say that," he said. He thought he sounded very modest.

"I'd like to see you skate sometime," she said.

He shrugged. "Sure."

"Have you gotten a band together here?"

"A band?"

"Yeah, you said you played in a band before you moved here."

"Oh," Jerry said. "Yes, I did. You have a very good memory."

"What do you play?"

His mind leaped back to some of the articles on rock music he'd studied over the summer.

"Guitar. Lead guitar."

Cinnamon smiled. "You must be good."

"Oh, I wouldn't say that," he said again. "But our *group* was pretty good. We had a few gigs last year, and we were going to cut a CD, but then I had to move."

No one listening would have any idea that Jerry had never held a guitar in his life. His research had really paid off. The lies were coming so easily, flowing effortlessly off his tongue. He was amazing himself.

"What was the name of your band?" Cinnamon asked him.

"Midnight Sun." He'd thought of it so fast!

"That's a good name. Do you write songs?"

"We're mostly a cover band," he said. "But I wrote some of our songs. Our band won a competition with one of my compositions."

"You wrote a song? What was it called?"

His mind leaped again and landed on one of Melissa's favorite books. "'Madeline.'"

Cinnamon smiled and tilted her head. "Is Madeline your girlfriend?"

He shrugged and put on a sad face. "It's over now."

Cinnamon's smile widened. "Maybe you'll write a song for someone *else*."

"Maybe."

The bell rang, startling them both. The hall around them was empty. Jerry hadn't even noticed that the kids had disappeared into classrooms.

"Second period's started already!" Jerry said.

Cinnamon squealed and they both ran to Ms. Robertson's room and flew in the door. The other kids giggled when he and Cinnamon returned together. There were even some *Oooooo*s called out from the back.

Jerry hardly noticed, though. His head was filled with thoughts of Cinnamon, beautiful Cinnamon, who had talked to him and smiled and asked him questions about himself.

She seemed awfully impressed with him. He let himself fantasize that maybe she was changing her mind about who her goal would be this year. It seemed totally impossible that beautiful Cinnamon O'Brien could have any interest in him, Jerry Flack, the dork. But stranger things had happened. And it was wonderful dreaming about it.

He replayed his conversation with her in his mind. A stray thought tugged at him. He pushed it away, not wanting anything to tarnish this moment of happiness. But the thought came back and nagged at him and wouldn't leave him alone. He finally turned his mind toward the thought and gave it his grudging attention.

Okay, so the lies were piling up fast.

*Jerry had gone hang gliding with his dog. He'd met Leonardo DiCaprio. He was an expert skater. He played lead guitar in a band and wrote songs. His old girlfriend was named Madeline.*

Would he remember all the lies he'd told? Would that tangled web finally trip him up, so he'd fall flat on his face in front of the cool crowd?

Jerry took a deep breath and slid down in his seat. He didn't feel so wonderful now.

How could he keep his disguise in place? How long could he pretend? He didn't know, but it was too late to turn back.

Maybe he'd better buy some more teen magazines on his way home. Maybe he just needed to study some more. And maybe he should keep a list of the lies he'd told so he wouldn't forget.

It sure was getting complicated.

# Chapter Eight

r. Hooten walked into the classroom and took something out of his pocket. He pushed his thumb into the end of it, and a loud shriek blasted from it.

Jerry jumped in his seat, several people screamed, and everyone covered their ears.

Mr. Hooten grinned and turned off the noise. "Gets your attention, doesn't it?"

"Geez, Mr. Hooten," either Kim or Kat Henley said, several rows back. "Give us a warning, will you, before you ruin our eardrums?"

"What was that?" asked her sister.

"It's a stimulus," said Mr. Hooten. "We're going to be talking about stimuli. Actually, this particular stimulus is called a Shrieker. You can carry it with you. If you're attacked, you just push this button. Why do you think it works?"

Brenda raised her hand. "It draws attention."

"It sure does," Mr. Hooten said. He held up the small device. "A stimulus is any change in the environment around an organism that produces a response. What was your response?"

"We jumped," Jerry said.

"About a foot in the air," Mr. Hooten said, grinning. "You should've seen it—you all looked pretty funny. But you're right. A response is an action." He looked around the room. "What would be another example of a stimulus?"

"The smell of popcorn when I walk into a movie theater," Kat Henley said. "My response is that my mouth waters."

"Terrific," Mr. Hooten said. "Someone give me another example."

"Sunlight is a stimulus," Chad Newsome said.

"Explain," responded Mr. Hooten.

"Plants grow toward the sun."

"Excellent."

Another stimulus, Jerry thought, is Cinnamon O'Brien. She makes my heart pound hard.

Jerry thought again how glad he was that Cinnamon, Gabe, and Craig weren't in Mr. Hooten's class. It would've been awfully hard to pretend that he wasn't interested in science. He wasn't sure about Tony, who *was* in his class. He didn't know if Tony would report back to the others. Tony was pretty quiet, though, so maybe Jerry wouldn't have to worry about it.

After class, Mr. Hooten asked Jerry to stay behind for a minute.

"Jerry," he said, after the rest of the students had left, "I've had a look at your records from your previous school. Ms. Robertson and I are coaches for the sixth-grade science team. We'd like you to consider joining."

"What is it?"

"We study different aspects of science, quiz one another, and compete as a team against other schools. Our first competition will be held in a few weeks, so we have to get started. It's a lot of fun."

"Who else is on it?" Jerry asked.

"So far, just the Henley sisters."

Of course, Jerry thought. Brenda had said they were very smart. Besides, they were each about as dorky as a person can get.

It takes one to know one.

"I'm going to ask Brenda McAdams to join the team," Mr. Hooten said. "And we'll ask Chad Newsome, too, and a few other good students."

He paused a moment, then said, "You don't need to give me an answer now. But think about it. You'd be an asset to the team. And you'd like it; we have a good time."

"I'll think about it," Jerry said.

Mr. Hooten nodded and smiled. "See you tomorrow."

Out in the hall, the Henley sisters were waiting. Kim asked, "Are you going to join the science team? Mr. Hooten said he would ask you. We're going to have such a great time!"

Kat came up behind her sister. "We'll cut those other teams down to size, won't we, Jerry?"

"We don't even know yet whether he's going to join," Kim said to Kat.

"Why wouldn't he join?" Kat asked.

"How should I know?" Kim said. "Why don't you ask him? He's standing right there in front of you."

"Why wouldn't you join?" Kat asked him.

"Uh, I'm not sure," Jerry said. "I'm thinking about it."

"Chad's joining," Kim said.

"Oh," Jerry said. "Good. Well, see you."

He hurried down the hall before either sister could say any more. He needed time to think. He walked down the hall, mulling over his problem.

He *really* wanted to be on the science team. But could he be on the team and still pull off his cool disguise? It would be very dangerous.

Jerry felt as if he were skating on thin ice, and if he made one false move, he'd go plunging into icy waters while the cool kids laughed at him from the shore.

But he wouldn't think about that now. After all, Cinnamon O'Brien seemed to like him. What more could a guy ask for?

He decided, as he headed down the hall, that it was awfully risky to join the science team. Maybe he'd better not try it.

He didn't want anything to jeopardize his chances with Cinnamon.

"Hi, Brenda."

"Hi."

Jerry hadn't been able to talk to her for the rest of the afternoon. She had arrived at their classes just before the bell and hurried out with other friends before he could speak to her. He couldn't wait to tell her about his great conversation with Cinnamon. Finally after school, he had found her at her locker.

Brenda pulled out two notebooks and a science book.

"You going home now?" Jerry had to talk loud over the banging lockers and yelling kids in the hall.

"Yup."

"I'll walk with you partway."

"Okay, sure."

"I wanted to tell you about the great conversation I had with Cinnamon today."

Brenda closed her locker and turned to Jerry.

"Oh. Sure. Congratulations."

"Thanks. I'm going to try and write a song for her. You think she'd like that?"

"Yeah, why wouldn't she?"

"Hey, thanks for suggesting that I be nice to her." Jerry grinned. "I don't know why I didn't think of it."

Brenda laughed. "Yeah, being nice—what a concept, right? Hey, I've got to go. I'm meeting Aubrey at my house after her flute lesson. We're going to listen to some CDs."

Disappointment flickered through Jerry and settled into his chest. He'd hoped that Brenda would be more excited about his success with Cinnamon. He had wanted her to ask him to recount the conversation, word for word. He had hoped she'd celebrate his victory with him. After all, she was his coach, the one who had given him such great advice.

"Could you wait for me?" Jerry asked. "I have to stop at my locker first."

"Well, okay, sure."

"Wait by the oak tree, okay?" Jerry said. "I'll be right there."

Jerry hurried to his locker, grabbed what he needed, and went outside.

Brenda wasn't standing by the tree. Jerry squinted and looked around, but he didn't see her.

"Hey, Flack!" Jerry turned to see Gabe right behind him.

"I thought you were 'sick,'" Jerry said.

"School's out," Gabe said, grinning. "So I'm suddenly feeling better."

Jerry thought he had a lot of nerve, showing up at school after being gone all day. What if a teacher saw him?

"Have you seen Cinnamon?" Gabe asked.

Jerry's heart stopped. "No, not since school got out."

"Hey, Gabe! Jerry!" Jerry squinted and saw blurry Cinnamon and fuzzy Robin gesturing to them at the corner of the building.

"Come on," Gabe said. Jerry followed him.

"Where are we going?" He looked around, searching for Brenda. Where was she, anyway?

On the sidewalk, at the top of the steep slope that led down to the playing field, a group of kids had gathered. Cinnamon, Robin, Tony, Carrie, Craig, and several others were talking and laughing.

"Have you ever skated down this hill, Gabe?" Robin asked.

"Not yet," Gabe answered.

Cinnamon was smiling at Gabe, so Jerry jumped in to get her attention. "It would be really awesome to rollerblade down that hill."

Gabe turned to Jerry. "So why don't you do it?"

"Me?" Jerry gulped.

"Great idea, Flack," Craig said. "I've been waiting to see you skate."

Everyone looked at Jerry. "I—I don't have my skates," he stammered.

Out the corner of his eye, he saw someone standing away from the crowd. He turned and saw a blurry Brenda. She was listening to the conversation.

"I've got rollerblades in my backpack," Gabe said. He grinned slyly. "Unless maybe you're scared?"

Jerry, feeling Cinnamon's eyes on him, forced a laugh. "Scared? Ha-ha. No way. But your skates wouldn't fit me. I've got big feet."

"What size?"

"A man's size seven and a half."

"Same as me." Gabe threw his backpack off his shoulder and opened it.

Jerry's knees were suddenly weak. What was he going to do now? How could he get out of this?

Gabe handed Jerry the skates. "Here you go."

Jerry's heart was slamming into his ribs. He felt light-headed. He reached out and took the skates. Everyone stared at him.

He knew he didn't have a choice. He would lose face if he didn't rollerblade down the hill. He had to do it, even if he was killed in the process.

"Okay." It came out a whisper.

Craig clapped. "Cool!"

"This'll be good," Robin said.

Jerry sat down and put on the skates. He heard

a cough and looked up to see Brenda edging nearer. She looked horrified.

He stood up and stepped carefully to the very edge of the hill.

He glanced back at Cinnamon, who looked very impressed. The guys also watched with great interest.

Jerry took a big breath—knowing it might well be his last—and pushed off the edge of the hill, his knees bent slightly.

He jerked to one side and the other. His arms began to flail wildly.

Then, a miraculous thing happened. Heading down the hill, he heard a voice in his head. It wasn't an angel's voice, but it was just as wonderful. He remembered reading a physics book he'd checked out of the library several months ago. *"A body is more stable when the center of gravity is lowered and there is a broad base of support."*

Jerry leaned forward slightly, bent his knees till he was squatting, and widened the distance between his feet.

He zoomed down the hill, picking up speed as he tore along the sidewalk.

He didn't fall.

Faster and faster he sped.

He was edging left. He couldn't control it.

The wind blew his hair.

His shirt flapped on his back.

*Zooom.*

He tore along at the left edge of the sidewalk.

He started to wobble.

Out of control.

He was at the bottom of the hill now and began to slow just as his left foot skated off the sidewalk.

He slammed into a tree and fell backward on his butt in the grass.

The world spun around him. His face hurt, his knees hurt, and his butt hurt. But that was okay.

*I didn't die*, Jerry thought happily.

He heard feet running down the sidewalk. He struggled to sit up. The kids surrounded him, slapping him on the back.

"He did it," Robin cried.

"What a great ride!" Craig whooped.

"You handled it like a pro," Gabe said.

Cinnamon knelt beside him and touched his cheek. "You're going to have a black eye, Jerry." She smiled and gazed at him. "Cool!"

Jerry smiled back at her. Because he knew now, without a doubt, he was in.

# Chapter Nine

"Did you see me fly down that hill?" Jerry asked. He was sitting on the floor in his parents' bedroom, talking on the phone. Sassy's head rested on his leg.

"I thought you were dead for sure," Brenda said. "I looked for you after it was over."

"After you smashed into the tree, I waited long enough to see you move. I knew you were alive, so I left. Besides, you were surrounded by all those kids."

Jerry laughed. "You should see my eye. It's getting black and blue—a real shiner. Hey, thanks a lot, Bren. You helped me get in with those kids. You know, the jeans ripping and the strut lessons and everything. I just hope I can keep up with the disguise. It's getting harder and harder." He reached over to scratch Sassy, and he winced. "Not to mention painful."

"Yeah, I bet," she said. "Oh, by the way, Mr. Hooten talked to me about the science team after school—that's why I was late—and he said he'd asked you, too. Are you going to join?"

"I don't think so," Jerry said. "I'm in with these kids now, and I don't want to mess it up."

"But you like science so much—" Brenda said.

"I know," Jerry said. "I wish I could do it. But if Cinnamon and Gabe found out, I'd have to work that much harder to convince them I'm cool. This is hard enough work as it is."

"If you say so."

"I'll see you tomorrow," Jerry said.

"See you."

Jerry hung up and went back to his bedroom, where the pieces of his hovercraft lay: the vacuum cleaner motor, the large round board with a hole in the middle, a large sheet of plastic, duct tape, and a box of utility staples.

"This is going to be so cool," Jerry murmured, settling down on the floor.

The phone rang, and a moment later Mrs. Flack called from downstairs, "Jerry, telephone! It's for you again!"

He ran back to his parents' bedroom.

"Hello?"

"Hi, Jerry. This is Cinnamon."

Jerry's stomach performed an impressive triple somersault. "Hi."

"I just wanted to call and see how you're doing," she said.

Jerry was suddenly fantastic, sensational, and ecstatic, but what he answered was, "Fine." He was playing it cool.

"You really hit that tree hard."

"I can take it."

"I know," Cinnamon said. "You were very brave to rollerblade down that hill."

"Well," he said in his most modest voice, "I've skated down hills steeper than that."

"Wow." There was a pause. "Jerry, do you know about the fall carnival at the high school?"

"A fall carnival?"

"Yeah. It's in a couple of weeks, and it's really fun. They have it every year. There are games and cotton candy and stuff. There's a dance, too, with a live band."

"Sounds great!" Jerry said.

"All the kids are going. You know, Robin, Gabe, Craig, Tony."

"Cool!"

"So you want to come with us?" Cinnamon asked. "It's the biggest thing of the fall."

"Sure."

"So what's with you and Brenda McAdams?"

"What do you mean?"

"Well, I've seen you talking with her. And don't you eat lunch with her?"

"Yeah," Jerry said. "Don't you like Brenda?"

"Oh, she's nice," Cinnamon answered. "But, well, she's just not cool, you know. I mean, she's so smart and kind of shows off her brains a lot."

"She shows off her brains?"

"Yeah, you know. She always has her hand in the air to answer the teachers' questions. And she uses really big words."

"I guess I hadn't noticed."

"Like the other day," Cinnamon said, "when we were talking about that story in language arts? She said the character *expired*. I didn't even know what that meant till I figured out it meant that he died!"

Jerry laughed. He thought it was funny and kind of cute that she didn't know what *expired* meant.

"I mean," Cinnamon said, "why couldn't she just say the guy *died*, for Pete's sake?"

"Or passed away?" Jerry said. "Or croaked?"

Cinnamon giggled. "Or kicked the bucket?"

"Or bought the farm?"

"I like that one," Cinnamon said. "Bought the farm. That sounds like something Gabe would say."

Jerry didn't want to talk about Gabe.

"Did you know Gabe skipped school today?" Cinnamon asked.

"Yeah," Jerry said. "I wonder if any of the teachers saw him after school?"

"Probably not," Cinnamon said. "He says he never gets caught." There was a pause. "He has dreamy hair."

"He does?"

"Yeah. And—" She giggled. "He's so sexy."

Jerry didn't know what to say. He said, "Oh."

"Well, my mom's calling me," Cinnamon said. "She probably wants me to help fix dinner." She sighed heavily. "What a pain. I hate cooking."

"Me, too." Actually, Jerry liked cooking, but it wouldn't be cool to admit it.

"I'll see you tomorrow at school," Cinnamon said. "Oh, and Jerry?"

"Yes?" He straightened up.

"Are you going to play your guitar tonight? Or write any songs?"

"I don't know," Jerry said. "You think I should write a song?"

"If you want to. Do I give you aspiration?"

"Aspiration?"

She laughed. "There I go, using big words like Brenda. You know, do I make you want to write songs?"

"Oh, sure," Jerry said. "You really give me aspiration."

Cinnamon giggled. "Good. See you tomorrow, Jerry."

"Bye."

Jerry hung up the phone. Adrenaline was still streaking through his body. He couldn't believe that Cinnamon O'Brien had actually called him on the phone!

Except for the part about Gabe's being sexy, the conversation had been a good one. So what if she said *aspiration* instead of *inspiration*? And didn't know what *expire* meant? It wasn't a big deal that she didn't have much of a vocabulary.

She wanted him to go to the carnival!

She wanted him to write a song for her, too, that was obvious. He couldn't read a note of music, but maybe he could write a poem. After all, that's what songs are, poems set to music.

He went to his room, walked past the hovercraft materials on the floor, and sat at his desk to start working on a song for Cinnamon.

"Does it hurt a lot?" Mrs. Flack asked at dinner.

"Not much," Jerry said, touching his black eye.

"Looks like you were hit pretty hard," Mr. Flack said.

"Have some potatoes, Jerry," Mrs. Flack said. "You say you ran into a tree?"

"Mmm." Jerry didn't want to talk about it. He took the bowl from his mother.

"Did you ever find the paper today, Claire?" Mr. Flack asked, sawing at his baked chicken.

"Eventually," she said, rolling her eyes. "I'm giving Angie Lennox one more chance. If she doesn't throw the newspaper on the porch or somewhere in plain sight tomorrow afternoon, I'm going to call her supervisor."

"I think we should train Sassy to find it and put it on the porch," Jerry said. "That might be easier in the long run."

Mr. Flack stopped eating, and Mrs. Flack's eyes opened wide.

"Are you kidding? I thought Sassy was untrainable," Mrs. Flack said. "She's always up to something! Remember when she collected one shoe from every pair of shoes in the house, and she piled them in the middle of the living room?"

"She could learn to bring the paper," Jerry said. "I've been reading about positive reinforcement in the training of laboratory rats."

"Sassy's not a rat!" Melissa cried.

"We'll start after supper," Jerry said. "Do you have a newspaper I can use?"

"Sure," his mother answered. "But Jerry, don't get your hopes up."

"She'll learn," Jerry said.

"This'll be fun!" Melissa said.

"I just hope it works," said Mrs. Flack.

After supper, Jerry and Melissa began Sassy's training.

"Okay, Sassy," Jerry said. "Bring the paper."

"Bring it here, Sassy," Melissa said, sitting on the front step.

"We should always use the same words so she won't be confused," Jerry said. "Let's say, 'Bring the paper.'"

"Bring the paper, Sassy."

Jerry had dropped the paper, folded with a rubber band around it, by the evergreens under the front windows. Now he tugged on Sassy's leash and led her to the paper. He squatted down in front of her, pried her mouth open, and gently slid the paper between her teeth.

"Bring the paper, Sassy," Jerry said. He led her up the steps to the front door and took the paper from her mouth.

"Good girl," Jerry said. "Here's your positive reinforcement." He petted her, then took a doggy treat out of his pocket and gave it to her. Sassy devoured it on the spot. After the treat was gone, Sassy looked up at Jerry, swinging her tail back and forth.

"She wants to do it again," Melissa said.

"Okay," Jerry said. "Melissa, put the paper in a different place."

Melissa ran and dropped the paper on the other side of the sidewalk.

Jerry and Melissa practiced with Sassy for an hour. During the last fifteen minutes, Melissa hid the paper under the shrubbery, and Jerry and Sassy had to look for it.

"Think she's catching on?" Melissa asked.

"Maybe," Jerry said. "But it'll be a while before she'll do it on her own." He patted Sassy's head. "I've got some important business to do now."

"What's that?"

"I'm writing a song."

Melissa brightened. "Can I help write it?"

"No," Jerry said. "This is a special song for a special person."

"Yeah, so?"

"So I have to write it myself. You don't know anything about song writing."

"Neither do you," Melissa said.

Jerry sighed. "I'm not letting a dumb six-year-old mess up my song, okay?"

Melissa scowled and ran in the house. "Mo-om! Jerry called me 'dumb'!"

Jerry shook his head. Sometimes it was hard for a cool sixth grader to put up with such immaturity.

He went inside and up to his room to work on the song that he hoped might possibly win Cinnamon's heart.

# Chapter Ten

$J$erry strutted onto the school grounds Friday morning. His cool walk was becoming so natural to him now that it took only four steps to get warmed up.

Jerry stopped by Mr. Hooten's room early. His teacher's eyes widened when he saw him. "How did you get that shiner, Jerry?" he asked.

"I had a rollerblading accident," Jerry said.

"Ouch!"

Jerry told him he wouldn't be joining the science team.

"I'm sorry to hear that," Mr. Hooten said. "If there's a problem with transportation, we could arrange for a car pool among the parents. Maybe

Ms. Robertson and I could help, too."

Jerry felt a stab of guilt.

"Uh, thanks, but that isn't the problem," he said. "I just . . . I just . . . don't think I'll have time."

"Well, okay," Mr. Hooten said. "We'll miss you. You would have been a valuable addition to the team." He smiled, and Jerry almost changed his mind on the spot. He forced himself to think of Cinnamon, her red hair and clear blue eyes.

"Thanks," Jerry said. "Maybe next year."

Mr. Hooten laughed. "I think our sixth-grade competitors would take a dim view of our having a seventh grader on the team."

"Oh, yeah." A lump formed in his stomach. This would be his last chance to be on the science team. But he'd made his decision. "Well," he said, looking at the floor, "see you."

Jerry hurried down the hall to his locker and pulled out the books for his morning classes. If only there was a way that he could be cool *and* be on the science team.

Craig appeared, leaned against the next locker, and grinned. "Cool shiner, Flack."

"I heard about the carnival," Jerry said. "Cinnamon said we'd all go together."

Craig grinned. "Yeah. It's pretty cool."

"Cinnamon said everybody will be there."

"You mean, everybody *cool* will be there."

Jerry grinned. "Everybody *cool*, of course."

Cinnamon, Robin, and Gabe appeared. "Look at that shiner!" Robin whooped.

Cinnamon grinned.

"Hey, Flack," Robin said. "Cinnamon told me you're going to the carnival with us. You haven't *lived* till you've been to the fall carnival."

"Sounds cool," Jerry said. "Are you girls walking to language arts now?"

"Sure," Cinnamon said. "Come on."

Cinnamon and Robin strolled next to Jerry while he strutted down the hall. The girls hadn't even invited Gabe, who was also in the class. They'd just left him standing there with Craig. Jerry decided that was a *very* good sign.

Several sixth graders turned to watch them. Jerry loved it. He was sure they were wishing they could join this cool threesome.

Yes, he thought. He'd made the right choice. The science team could never be as much fun as this.

Brenda looked up when Jerry walked in with Cinnamon and Robin. She smiled at him. "Hi, Flack," she said as he sat down behind her. "That eye sure looks bad."

"Thanks."

Brenda leaned in, grinning, and began to sing very quietly, "Happy birthday to me, happy birthday to me—"

"It's your birthday today?" Jerry asked, grinning at her.

She continued to smile. "Yes indeedy."

"Happy birthday, Brenda."

"Thanks. My best present was a new computer game. You want to come over after school and play it with me?"

"What game is it?"

"Alien Abductors. It's really cool. See, these aliens are coming to Earth and abducting kids, and—"

"I've heard that's an awesome game," Jerry said. "Yeah, I'll walk home with you."

Brenda beamed. "Great. See you at lunch."

"Yeah, see you."


Jerry stopped at his locker before lunch, dropped off his morning books, and picked up his afternoon books and notebooks.

"What's new, Jerry?"

He turned to see Cinnamon standing next to him.

His heart leaped and he grinned at her. "None of your business."

Cinnamon burst out laughing. "You're so funny, Jerry!" She leveled her clear blue eyes at him. "Did you write a song last night?"

"I worked on one."

"What's the name of it?"

"Wait till it's finished," Jerry said, smiling slyly. "Then I'll let you see it."

She gave him a playful shove. "You're so mean, keeping me in suspense."

"It won't be long," he said, breathless that she'd touched him.

"You going down to lunch?"

"Yup."

She walked alongside him down the stairs toward the cafeteria. Once her arm brushed his, and he nearly jumped out of his skin. He'd never felt that kind of thrill before. It was even better than the shove she'd given him. If this had been one of those corny Broadway musicals his mother liked to listen to, he would have burst into song at that moment. *"Her arm touched mine, and I felt so divine! And I knew in a flash that she soon would be mine!"*

The first person they saw inside the cafeteria was Gabe Marshall.

"Hi, Gabe," Cinnamon called and twiddled her fingers at him.

Great, Jerry thought. There are probably two hundred kids in the cafeteria right now, and we have to run into Gabe Marshall.

Gabe swaggered over and stood next to Cinnamon.

"What's new?" she asked.

"Nothin'."

Jerry smiled to himself. At least he'd had a funny answer to that question that had made Cinnamon laugh. He wondered if Cinnamon noticed that Gabe's answer wasn't as good as his.

Jerry looked up slightly at Gabe. For the first time, he noticed that Gabe was about an inch taller than he was. He hoped Cinnamon hadn't noticed. He took a step toward Cinnamon and stood as tall as his spine would stretch.

"Did you know that Jerry writes songs?" Cinnamon asked Gabe.

Gabe glanced at Jerry. "No, I didn't."

"And he's working on a new one," Cinnamon said.

Jerry smiled at her. "I think it's one of my best."

Craig appeared next to Jerry. "Get in line, Marshall, I'm starved. Hey, Flack, come and sit with us."

Jerry walked with Craig, Gabe, and Cinnamon through the lunch line, picked up his food, and sat at Gabe's table with Craig and Tony. Cinnamon left to eat with Robin and Carrie.

"So who's going to the carnival with us?" Craig asked.

"I don't care," Gabe said. "As long as Cinnamon's going." Jerry stopped chewing and stared at Gabe. Gabe turned to Jerry and gave him a meaningful look. "I think she likes me."

Craig laughed loudly. "She practically drools over you, Marshall."

Gabe grinned directly at Jerry. "Yeah, she does, doesn't she?"

"But," Craig said, "she was real impressed with Flack's rollerblading. You see her touch his face after he hit the tree? Ooooo! I thought she might *kiss* him."

"Yeah, right," Gabe said sarcastically.

"She called me," Jerry said casually, "to see how I was doing."

Gabe's eyebrows shot up. "She called you?"

"Yeah," Jerry said. He shrugged, watching Gabe. "She's nice."

Gabe stabbed viciously at a meatball on top of his spaghetti.

A little voice in Jerry's head cautioned him to be quiet, but he kept rattling on. "I'm writing a song that I think she'll like. She says she can't wait for me to finish it. It's called 'Cinnamon.'"

"Is that right?" Gabe said. He glared at Jerry, and Jerry saw the muscles tighten in his jaw.

There was a long, tense silence.

Craig did the only talking during the rest of lunch. Gabe sat stone-silent and angry, and Jerry shoved the spaghetti down his throat, not tasting it at all and wishing he hadn't said what he'd said.

Only Tony seemed to notice. He sat quietly and glanced back and forth between Jerry and Gabe.

Jerry did *not* need a war with Gabe. Sure, Cinnamon seemed to like Jerry a lot, but she had also talked about Gabe's dreamy hair. And she'd called him *sexy*.

Jerry wondered if maybe he should have let Brenda make the sexy tears in his jeans, just below the pockets.

Brenda! That's when he remembered. He'd said he'd see her at lunch; he was supposed to sit with her today. It was her birthday.

He half-stood and looked out over the blurry sea of faces in the cafeteria. He spotted her right away, sitting with the fuzzy-maned Henley sisters and Aubrey Lane.

Jerry couldn't see her clearly, but he could tell that she was talking with her friends.

"I gotta go," Jerry said.

He stepped over the bench, headed directly to Brenda's table and sat backwards in the empty space next to her.

"Hey, Brenda," he said. "I'm sorry I didn't eat with you. Especially since it's your birthday."

Brenda glanced at him. "It's okay," she said and shrugged. She turned back to the Henley sisters. "Anyway, I thought the movie was great!"

Kat Henley rolled her eyes. "It was a horrible story! I hate sad endings."

Jerry leaned in closer. "I don't know how it happened. I just forgot about having lunch with you. See, Cinnamon stopped at my locker, and as soon as we walked in here, we saw Gabe—"

Brenda turned to him and frowned. "I told you, Flack, it's all right. So *forget* it, okay? Just drop it."

She turned her back on him and started up her conversation again.

Jerry could tell that Brenda was ticked off. And why wouldn't she be? She'd helped him tear his jeans, worked on his strut with him, and given him great advice on how to be cool. She'd been a good friend.

And then he forgot to sit with her at lunch on her birthday.

The bell rang, and everyone got up and started for the door.

"Wait, Brenda," he said.

Brenda turned to him impatiently. "*What already?*"

"I really am sorry."

She sighed. "It's all right; I'll get over it. It's not a big deal. Really. See you later."

She gave him a little wave and walked away with Kim, Kat, and Aubrey.

Jerry stood and watched her go and felt a space hollow out in his chest. He hoped he hadn't blown it with Brenda. She was about the nicest person he'd met since moving to Spencer Lake, and he didn't want to lose her.

# Chapter Eleven

*J*erry tried all afternoon to get Brenda's attention so he could talk to her, but she walked out of every class with Kim and Kat Henley and Aubrey Lane.

He watched her, and hour by hour, the loneliness grew inside him.

After school, he went to Brenda's locker and waited for fifteen minutes. She didn't arrive. Maybe, he thought, she had already stopped at her locker and was on the way home.

He remembered she'd said she lived on Robin Hood Road. He went to the public phone on the wall near the front door and looked up her house number.

He trudged all the way there, forgetting about the cool swagger he'd perfected. He was going to say he'd come to play Alien Abductors. After all, she had invited him. Maybe they'd have lots of fun, and they'd be good friends again by the end of the afternoon.

Brenda's house was large and white with black shutters and a big porch that wrapped around the front. A swing hung from the porch ceiling. He climbed the steps and knocked.

A few moments later, the door opened. Brenda smiled when she saw him.

"Hey, Flack."

"Hi. I just thought I'd come over and play Alien Abductors. And say happy birthday again."

"Oh, thanks."

Jerry glanced at the swing. "You want to sit for a minute? I like these old porch swings."

"Okay." Brenda sat in the swing on one end. Jerry planted himself next to her, pushed back with his feet, then let go and swung forward.

"We have our first science team meeting tomorrow," Brenda said, staring off at a tree in the distance. "It's going to be so much fun. Mr. Hooten says that after the out-of-town competitions, we get to go out for pizza before we come home."

Jerry shook his head. "I wish I could be on the team. You guys are going to have a great time."

Brenda didn't say anything but continued to

stare off as if she were imagining the cool time she'd have with her friends.

Jerry folded his arms. "This is so dumb, Bren. I shouldn't have to give up the science team to be cool. Maybe I could pull it off. Maybe the cool kids wouldn't even find out I'm on it."

"Are you really thinking about joining the team?" Brenda asked, turning to him.

"Yeah," Jerry said. "In fact, I've decided. I don't want to miss out."

Brenda grinned. "Great. It'll be so much more fun with you there, Flack."

Jerry smiled. He was relieved that he and Brenda were still friends. But he had a new, awful feeling nagging at him. Things with Cinnamon and the cool kids were still so shaky. What would happen if they found out he was on the science team? And what would he do then?

"She's never going to get it!" Melissa cried.

She sat on the front stoop, her elbows resting on her knees.

"Yes, she will," Jerry said. "Okay, Sassy. Bring the paper."

He guided Sassy on the leash over to the shrub. Melissa had hidden the paper just under the bottom branches so it would be easy for Sassy to find it and pick it up.

"Bring the paper, girl."

Sassy wagged her tail and looked up at Jerry with her tongue hanging out of her mouth. Jerry sighed, leaned down, and guided Sassy's head to the paper. "Bring the paper, Sassy."

He put the paper in Sassy's mouth. "Good girl. Bring the paper."

He led her to the porch, where Melissa pulled the paper out of her mouth. "Good girl," Melissa said, patting her head and giving her a doggy treat. "You're a good dog, even though you're awful dumb."

"She isn't dumb," Jerry said. "She'll get it." If she doesn't die of old age first, he thought.

"Hello, Cinnamon?" Jerry sat cross-legged on the floor in his parents' room and spoke into the phone, his heart thundering in his chest.

"Yes?"

"This is Jerry."

"Hi, Jerry."

"I finished my song and thought you might like to hear it."

Cinnamon squealed. "You're going to sing it for me over the phone?"

"Uh, no. I broke a guitar string and have to get it fixed. But I'll read you the lyrics."

"Just a minute." There was a muffled sound as if Cinnamon covered the mouthpiece with her hand. *Shut up, Jenny! I can't hear anything!* she screamed.

"Sorry, Jerry." Her voice was back again, and soft. "I couldn't hear you. My bratty little sister was making too much noise."

"Oh, that's okay," Jerry said. "You want me to read you the words to my song?"

"Sure."

"It's called 'Cinnamon.'"

"Oh, Jerry! I've never had someone write a song about me before!"

Jerry cleared his throat, held up the piece of lined notebook paper, and read:

*Cinnamon O'Brien,*

*I know you know her name.*

*Once you've act-u-ally seen her face,*

*You'll never be the same.*

*She's beautiful and popular,*

*The one who steals your heart.*

*She's used to getting valentines,*

*So bring hundreds in a cart.*


*Cinnamon O'Brien,*

*Sweetest of the group,*

*She'd do anything for a friend*

*Even make chicken soup.*

*Total-really awesome,*

*You can't sit on the fence,*

*One look from her,*

*You're stuck for sure.*

*You love her fashion sense.*


*Cinnamon O'Brien,*

*Prettiest by far,*

*Compare her to a flower,*

*Compare her to a star.*

*If only I could hold her,*

*Touch her face and hair,*

*Tell her she's the one for me,*

*And say how much I care.*


His hand shaking, Jerry put the paper on the floor. He was glad he'd decided to read the poem to Cinnamon over the phone. His face was so hot, his mother could've fried hash browns on it. He had never talked mushy to anyone before.

There was a long pause. Heavy silence hung in the air. Jerry was suddenly worried. Did she hate it? Why didn't she say anything?

"I had a little trouble with the rhythm in that first verse," he said. "So I used 'act-u-ally—'"

He heard a sniff.

"It's beautiful," she said. She sniffed again. "Really beautiful."

Jerry sighed, very relieved. "I'm glad you liked it. I've never really said stuff like this—"

"Jerry?"

"Yes?"

"Were you serious, about what you said in the song?"

Jerry cleared his throat. "Very serious."

"You really love my fashion sense?"

"Oh. Uh . . . yes. Yes, I do."

"Because I really try hard to be in fashion," she said. "The rest of the song was awesome, too. I can't wait to hear you sing it with the guitar. Could you bring me a copy of it on Monday?"

"Sure."

There was a muffled sound again on her end while she covered the mouthpiece. "Jenny, you're such a pain in the *butt*!" She came back on the line, her voice soft again. "Oh, sorry. It was my sister again."

"That's okay."

"Well, I'll see you Monday, Jerry. Thanks for the song. It was totally awesome."

"I'm glad you liked it."

Jerry hung up.

He had been nervous, but it had gone very well, he thought. Cinnamon was happy with her song.

She hadn't said anything about the mushy parts. Maybe she was as embarrassed as he was. But she'd said the song was awesome. And the song made her so happy that she cried.

Only once before had he done anything that made a person cry with happiness. That was when he was ten and gave his mother a poem he'd written about her in school for Mother's Day. In the poem, he'd written that she was the best mother in the solar system. She had hugged him tightly and cried, and he felt her tears on his cheek. He'd never seen his mother cry before, and it gave him a weird feeling.

This time, though, it wasn't weird. It was wonderful.

He decided that maybe he was beginning to understand women.

# Chapter Twelve

innamon ran up to Jerry Monday morning. "Jerry, did you bring the song with you?"

Jerry had been leaning against the oak, watching his blurry classmates mill around the school.

"Sure," he said. He reached into his book bag and took out a folded piece of lined notebook paper. He had copied it in his best masculine scrawl, but legibly, so she wouldn't have trouble reading it.

She took it from him, unfolded it, read it, and sighed. "This is so cool, Jerry," she said, sniffling. Her eyes were watery. "Thanks."

"You're welcome." Jerry smiled. The poem had brought tears to her eyes again!

Cinnamon sneezed, and then she sneezed again.

"Oh, shoot." She sniffled, took out a tissue, and blew her nose. "I've had this cold all weekend. It started Friday."

"Oh," Jerry said. "I hope you feel better soon."

Well, so what if the poem didn't make her cry? She obviously loved it.

"Thanks." Cinnamon turned and ran to Robin and Carrie, who were waiting next to the flagpole. Jerry watched Cinnamon hold the paper up and read the poem aloud to them. He couldn't hear her words, but he could hear her voice mixed among the hundreds of other voices on the school grounds.

He watched the blurry faces of Robin and Carrie. They grinned and sighed as Cinnamon read. Then they leaned forward, and Robin whooped loudly. She and Carrie applauded and laughed.

*Laughed.*

Jerry turned away, feeling his face heat up. Once he'd had a dream that he was naked at school, and this was almost as bad. Had he made a big mistake?

He knew that Cinnamon loved the poem. She'd said so herself. He just wished she hadn't shown it to anyone else.

"Great song, Jerry."

Cinnamon, Robin, and Carrie had appeared at his side. It was Robin who had spoken.

"Thanks," Jerry said.

The three girls giggled. "Real romantic," Robin

said. She glanced back at Cinnamon and grinned.

Jerry stood on one foot and then the other. He shrugged. "The most successful songs express emotions." That was a good response. It sounded professional.

"But the part about making chicken soup?" Carrie said. "You could tell Cinnamon she'd win a million dollars if she could make a good piece of toast, and she'd burn it."

"That's not true!" Cinnamon said, laughing. She looked over Jerry's shoulder and waved. "Hi, Gabe."

Oh, no, Jerry thought. The last person he wanted to see at this moment was Gabe.

"Jerry wrote a song for me," Cinnamon said, beaming up at Gabe, waving the paper in front of her. "It's really cool."

*Don't show it to him.*

"Real romantic," Carrie said.

*Don't read it to him.*

"Unbelievably romantic," Robin said. There was more than a trace of a smirk on her lips.

"It's a very nice song," Cinnamon said, stepping up next to Jerry.

"Let's see it," Gabe said.

*Don't!* Jerry's stomach tightened. He was sure Gabe would read it out loud and make fun of it all over school.

"No, I don't think I'll show it to you," Cinnamon

said, still smiling and holding the paper behind her back.

Jerry was surprised but terribly relieved.

Gabe scowled. "Who cares? It's just a stupid song."

"It isn't stupid," Cinnamon said, frowning. "It's beautiful."

Gabe waved his arm in disgust and stalked off.

Cinnamon stood and watched him for a long moment. "Robin, Carrie, come with me a minute," she said. She led them away into the crowd of kids.

The bell rang a few moments later, and Jerry strode in to the school building. He hoped that would be the end of the song. Maybe Cinnamon would just take it home and enjoy it by herself.

"Hey, Flack," Brenda said, racing up to him, just inside the building. "Let's go tell Mr. Hooten the good news."

"What good news?"

"That you're going to be on the science team!"

"Let's wait," Jerry said. "I don't want him to say anything about it in class."

"Oh, yeah," Brenda said, rolling her eyes. "I forgot, it's a big secret."

Fifteen minutes later, when language arts class began, Ms. Robertson asked the students to open their reading texts to page 45.

"Hey, Ms. R.," Gabe shouted from the back.

"We've got a writer right here in this class."

Giggles exploded from the girls sitting around Gabe. Ms. Robertson looked up at Gabe.

"What do you mean?"

*Oh, no.*

"Jerry Flack," Gabe said. "He wrote a song for Cinnamon."

Jerry looked down at his desk, his heart thundering.

Ms. Robertson glanced at Jerry, then at Gabe and Cinnamon.

"That's nice," she said. "I'm sure it's very special."

"I think Cinnamon should read it out loud," Gabe said.

The kids applauded. "Yeah!" they shouted. "Let's hear the song!"

"No, no, no!" Cinnamon said, laughing. "It's a very cool song, but I'm not going to read it." She held the notebook paper in front of her on the desk.

"*I'll* read it!" Robin said, jumping up. She grabbed the paper from Cinnamon's desk.

"No," Cinnamon said. "Don't read it." But she didn't sound as if she meant it.

"Robin, sit down, please," Ms. Robertson said. "This is not the time or the place."

"Oh, okay," Robin said, grinning. Just before she sat down, she said, "But it has something to do with wanting to *hold* Cinnamon and touch her face and hair!"

Whoops and whistles filled the classroom.

"Oooooo! Flack is so romantic!" Gabe shouted. "I never knew he had it in him!"

Heat pulsated in Jerry's face. He'd never felt so humiliated. He'd poured his heart out in the poem, and everyone was making fun of it.

"Look at him blush!" Robin cried, clapping gleefully.

"Okay, that's enough," Ms. Robertson said, holding up her hands. "Robin, I think you should have consulted with Cinnamon before you quoted from the song. After all, it's Cinnamon's song."

"Oh, that's okay," Cinnamon said, waving her hand. She glanced sideways at Gabe. "Jerry was really great to write it for me."

Jerry was glad to hear Cinnamon say those words. But somehow it didn't make him feel any better. He turned around and looked at Cinnamon, and then he knew why.

She was leaning on her hand, head cocked to the side, smiling over at Gabe.

Jerry had an awful feeling that Cinnamon's happiness with the song might have as much to do with Gabe as it did with him.

# Chapter Thirteen

"Do you think Cinnamon really likes me?" Jerry asked Brenda. They sat on the floor in his room, their science team papers spread out around them.

"How *couldn't* she like you?" Brenda asked. "She's always hanging out with you. And you wrote her a song and risked your life rollerblading down a hill for her—"

"But I wonder if she thinks I'm cool?"

Brenda thought a moment. "Well, she thought it was cool that you rollerbladed down a hill, smashed into a tree, and gave yourself a black eye."

"Yeah." Jerry sighed. "Acting cool sure is tough. I still have bruises."

"Yeah," Brenda said, "this whole Make-Jerry-Look-Cool project has been complicated." She looked at the papers spread out on the floor. "But so are these questions! The first competition is only two weeks away, and I hear the two other middle schools have very smart players. We'd better get back to work."

"Okay."

Brenda flipped through one of the books Ms. Robertson and Mr. Hooten had given them to study. "Here's another question."

"Okay," Jerry said. "Shoot."

"What is Newton's first law of motion?"

"Newton's first law states that any body moving uniformly in a straight line or in a state of rest will remain in that state unless it's acted on by some outside force."

"Great," Brenda said. "What about his second law?"

"That's easy," Jerry said. "I learned about that with my hovercraft."

Brenda's eyes lit up. "Is it finished? Let me see it!"

Jerry opened his closet door and rolled the large wooden disk across the hardwood floor. "This is the underside. See, I've stapled this heavy plastic to the wood so it completely covers the bottom."

"Why are there holes cut out of the plastic?" Brenda asked.

"The vacuum cleaner motor is attached on the top side and blows air through a hole in the wood and into the plastic. The only way the air can escape is through the cutouts in the plastic and out against the floor. So the air forces the disk up off the floor. Here, sit on it and hold on." Jerry laid the wooden disk flat on the floor.

Brenda sat cross-legged in the middle of the disk and grabbed hold of the metal handles.

"Ready?" Jerry plugged in the cord to the vacuum motor.

A loud blast, sounding like the biggest trombone in the universe, burst from the hovercraft, and Brenda was lifted an inch off the hardwood floor.

"Cool!" she shouted, her voice barely audible over the noise. Jerry gave the hovercraft a light push. The disk drifted over and bumped against his desk chair.

"Turn off the motor," Jerry hollered. Brenda flipped the switch, and the craft settled onto the floor.

"That was fun!" she said.

"It'll be more fun when I get a long extension cord," he said. "Then we'll be able to move farther while hovering."

"So you learned about Newton's second law with that?"

"Yeah," Jerry said. "Newton's second law tells what happens when a force is applied to an object.

The greater the force, the greater the acceleration of the object. The greater the mass of the object, the smaller the acceleration. In other words, the harder I push you on the hovercraft, the faster you move. But if you weighed twice as much, you wouldn't move as fast."

"Cool. What a great experiment. I can't wait till you show Mr. Hooten. Now you ask me a science question."

"What is Flack's first law?"

"Never heard of it."

"It's about being cool," Jerry said. "The greater the dorkiness in the kid, the less the kid will fit in with the cool crowd."

"You have a one-track mind, Flack."

"I know."


Jerry and Brenda practiced hard with the science team every afternoon for a week and a half. He had an elaborate strategy to keep anyone from finding out he was on the team. He didn't go to his locker or hang out in the hallway after school in case Craig or one of the others would stop him and invite him to go rollerblading or hang out. And he didn't wait in Mr. Hooten's room, either. Anybody could walk past and see him. The cool kids *never* hung out in the science room, and his disguise would be in serious jeopardy if somebody caught him there.

So every day after school, Jerry went into the

boys' bathroom and sat in one of the stalls and studied his science books and articles for ten minutes while the halls cleared. He hated it. But there was no place else he could go to avoid being found out.

His plan worked until the Wednesday before the first science team competition. That day, he'd waited the necessary ten minutes in the bathroom, then collected his things and walked out into the hall.

Standing together near the drinking fountain were Cinnamon, Robin, Gabe, Craig, and Tony.

"There's Jerry!" Cinnamon called out.

Normally, Jerry would have been thrilled that she called to him while she was standing with Gabe. But now, on his way to science team practice, he froze.

"Hey, Flack, come here," Craig yelled.

Jerry walked over to them on shaky legs.

"We're all going to the mall," Craig said. "Gabe's gonna look at rollerblades, and I'm gonna get some CDs. You wanna come?"

"Yeah, Jerry," Cinnamon said, smiling and gazing into his eyes. "Come with us."

Jerry's stomach did a flip-flop when his eyes met Cinnamon's. For a brief moment, he considered skipping the science team practice.

But he couldn't do that. His teammates were counting on him. Besides, he *liked* being on the team. He was having fun. And the competition was only three days away, on Saturday afternoon. The team had a lot of work to do.

"Uh, no, I can't," Jerry said.

"How come?" Craig asked.

"Oh. Well, I told my mom—" No, he thought, that sounds dorky. "Uh, I mean, I need to be home when my sister gets there. To baby-sit, you know. Geez, I hate it."

"No problem," Gabe said, obviously glad that Jerry wasn't coming.

"Yeah, no problem," Robin echoed. Jerry had a feeling that she'd never liked him.

"Okay, well, you can walk part of the way with us," Craig said. "Haven't I seen you walk home that way?"

"Oh." Jerry didn't know what to say. "Well, yeah."

"So come on," Craig said.

Craig and the others started walking, and Jerry couldn't think of how to get out of joining them. If he said he had to stop at his locker, they'd just stop with him. And he'd already said he had to go home now to watch his sister.

Jerry walked down the hall with them, hanging back, wishing he could turn around and go back to Mr. Hooten's classroom.

Ms. Robertson came toward them, nearly running up the hall, late for science team practice. Jerry hung his head and walked directly behind

Gabe. She didn't see him and hurried past.

On the way out the front door, Tony walked alongside Jerry.

"I thought you were on the science team," Tony said to him.

Jerry was startled. Gabe, Cinnamon, Robin, and Craig were walking and talking in front of them and didn't hear Tony's question.

"Uh, no!" Jerry said in a low voice. "Why would I be on the—why would I do that?"

"I saw you go in the science room after school about a week ago," Tony said. He shrugged. "I just thought maybe you were on the team."

"No way," Jerry said.

Tony didn't ask any more questions. They walked six more blocks before Jerry could leave them.

"I turn here," he said. "See you tomorrow."

"See you, Flack," Craig said. "Remember the carnival's this weekend."

Jerry remembered. It was Saturday evening after the science team competition.

"Yeah," Cinnamon said. "We're all meeting at the Ferris wheel at 6:30."

"I'll be there," Jerry said.

Cinnamon giggled. "We'll have fun!"

"Bye, Jerry," Tony said. He gave Jerry a little wave, and Jerry wondered if Tony had told the others that he thought Jerry was on the science team.

They moved on toward the mall.

Jerry walked a half block toward home, then doubled back, jogging through backyards toward Hawthorne School.

He'd be late, but he had saved his disguise.

It had been a very close call.

# Chapter Fourteen

"Jerry!" Melissa burst into his bedroom. It was Friday, the evening before the science competition and carnival. Science notes were spread all over Jerry's bed. "Come quick!"

"What happened?"

"Just come here!" Melissa hopped up and down and beckoned him to follow.

The heavy front door was standing open. Through the screen door Jerry could see Sassy's tail waving back and forth.

Jerry pushed the door open.

"Look! She finally understands!" Melissa said, pointing.

Their newspaper lay in the middle of the stoop, at Sassy's feet.

"She fetched the paper!"

Jerry grinned. "Good girl, Sassy. Good girl!" He stroked Sassy's head.

Sassy danced around Jerry's legs with her mouth slightly open and her tongue hanging out. Jerry thought she looked as if she were smiling and very proud of herself.

"Melissa, let's give her a doggy treat." Melissa raced back into the house.

Jerry gazed at Sassy. She's just like me, he thought. She learned something new and transformed herself. She isn't the mischievous, untrainable dog anymore; she's a helper dog who will find and bring us the paper.

Jerry grinned, his heart bursting with pride. Anything is possible!

"I'm so nervous," Brenda said, "I could throw up."

"We're about as ready as we can be," Jerry said. He looked in the mirror on the wall of the high school band room and straightened his tie.

In a few minutes, the sixth-grade science team competition would begin. Kim and Kat Henley and Chad Newsome huddled over the piano a few feet away and quizzed each other in low voices.

Hawthorne's competitors from Laura Ingalls Wilder Middle School and Louisa May Alcott Middle School paced around the room.

Brenda leaned in. "See that girl with the long dark braid? That's who we have to watch out for. Olivia Corning. She goes to Wilder, and she's practically a genius. I also hear she's a blue-ribbon snot."

"Yeah," Kat Henley said. "She holds her nose so high in the air, you can look right up her nostrils."

Ms. Robertson approached them.

"We're about ready to start," she said, smiling. "You've all worked very hard. No matter how we do in the competition, I want you to know that Mr. Hooten and I are very proud of you." Jerry and the others grinned.

Ms. Robertson turned to face the students from the other schools. "Okay, everyone," she called out. "It's time to assemble on the stage."

Jerry felt a new rush of adrenaline.

"This is it, guys," Brenda said. "Let's show 'em we're the best team around."

They all slapped hands.

The auditorium was about one-fourth filled with parents, teachers, and students. Jerry squinted at the audience and thought he saw his mom and dad in the center section. His mother waved a blurry hand, but he pretended not to see her. Even as a member of the science team, Jerry wasn't willing to be a total dork.

Jerry and his teammates sat at the table at stage right. The team from Alcott was in the middle, with Wilder on the left.

"Welcome to the sixth-grade science team competition," Mr. Meyer said, standing behind a lectern at stage right. "The students on these three teams have worked hard to get ready for this event. The questions have been drawn from a pool of five hundred science questions, grouped according to difficulty. For every correct answer, a point is earned. At the end of every round, the team with the fewest points is eliminated. There will be as many rounds as we need to determine a winner, with each round becoming more difficult."

Mr. Meyer gestured toward a bearded man sitting at a small table with a microphone. "Our judge is Professor Cotton, from the university physics department." Mr. Meyer glanced at the students onstage. "Everyone ready?"

The competitors nodded nervously.

"Let the competition begin," he said. He strode down the steps from the stage and sat next to Ms. Robertson and Mr. Hooten in the second row.

"The first question goes to Nathaniel Hawthorne Middle School," said Professor Cotton. Brenda was sitting at the end of the table, so it was hers. "'A group of organisms that are able to interbreed' is the definition of what term?"

Brenda smiled. "Species."

"Correct."

That was easy, Jerry thought, his heart pounding. He hoped his question would be that easy.

"Louisa May Alcott Middle School," said the professor, looking at the team in the middle of the stage. "There are seven major groups in scientific classification. What is the largest group?"

"Kingdom," said the boy sitting at the end of the table.

"Correct."

Another easy one. Maybe no one would make a mistake until the questions got harder.

"Laura Ingalls Wilder Middle School," Professor Cotton said. "They are called the building blocks of life and are the basic units of structure and function."

It was the easiest question yet. Olivia Corning, who sat on the right side of the table, rolled her eyes. "Cells, of course."

Brenda, sitting next to Jerry, nudged him. "What'd I tell you?" she whispered. "A blue-ribbon snot."

Now it was Jerry's turn.

"A pure substance that cannot, by ordinary means, be broken down into simpler substances is called what?"

"An element."

"Correct."

Jerry let out a breath. He'd gotten it right, but

then it had been a very simple question.

The rest of the questions in rounds one and two were so easy that no one made a mistake.

"Round three," said Professor Cotton.

Students shifted in their seats. These questions would be harder.

A door at the back of the auditorium swung open and a loud giggle drew everyone's attention. Jerry didn't have to have perfect vision to know who had just walked in. He'd recognize Cinnamon's laughter anywhere. The two fuzzy figures stopped short in the doorway as if they were surprised to see anyone in the auditorium.

"Oh, there's Jerry!" Jerry heard Cinnamon's voice loud and clear. "What's he doing up there?"

Gabe snorted and collapsed into a nearby seat. Cinnamon sat next to him.

Jerry was horrified. After all his work to keep it a secret, he'd finally been found out—and right in the middle of a competition!

Without even thinking about it, he slumped in his chair and threw his feet out under the table, assuming the Cool Guy posture he'd practiced so hard. Brenda glanced at him sharply.

"Hawthorne," the professor said. Brenda's head snapped around to listen to her question. "The siren of a moving ambulance seems to drop to a lower note as it passes. What is this phenomenon called?"

"The Doppler effect," she said.

"Correct."

"I knew that," Gabe said from the back, and Cinnamon laughed.

Mr. Meyer stood up and pointed at Gabe. It was a warning. Gabe grinned.

Brenda poked Jerry. "Sit up straight," she whispered. "Concentrate."

It was only then that Jerry realized his posture had changed, and all because Cinnamon had walked in. He sat up.

A few minutes went by as more questions were posed to the competitors.

Now it was Jerry's turn. He glanced at the back of the auditorium. Cinnamon and Gabe whispered, their heads together. They weren't even watching.

"Hawthorne," said the professor. "A pencil placed at an angle in a glass of water appears to bend at the surface because of what property of light?"

Jerry stared at Cinnamon and Gabe, whispering in the back. He couldn't see them very well, and his mind played tricks with his eyes. Their heads were so close. Were they *kissing* back there? He squinted, but he couldn't be sure.

"Hawthorne?" the professor said.

Brenda jabbed him in the ribs with her elbow.

Jerry jumped. "Hunh?"

"I'll repeat the question once," said the professor. "A pencil placed at an angle in a glass of water appears to bend at the surface because of what property of light?"

"Oh, refraction," Jerry said.

A loud giggle came from the back of the auditorium. "Oh, Gabe!" Cinnamon cried out.

Mr. Meyer bolted from his seat and strode swiftly to the back. He leaned over Cinnamon and Gabe and whispered to them. Then he opened the door behind him and ushered them out.

"Good riddance," said Brenda softly.

Jerry took a big breath and leaned forward in his seat. He wondered whether Cinnamon and Gabe would still want him to go to the carnival with them. But he had to put that thought out of his mind for now. He had almost cost his team a point!

At the end of the round, the professor said, "Alcott's team is down by one point. They are therefore eliminated."

Polite applause was offered to Alcott as they left the stage. Now it was just Hawthorne and Wilder.

"Round four," said Professor Cotton. "These questions will require more than a one-word or listing answer. You will be asked to explain various scientific properties and phenomena." Jerry heard Brenda take in a deep breath. These would be the really tough questions. "Again, the first question will be for Hawthorne."

"The first law of thermodynamics deals with energy. Please explain it."

Brenda nodded. "Energy is not created or destroyed. It's just changed from one form to another."

"Correct."

Brenda looked at Jerry and opened her eyes wide. She'd known the answer, but it was much harder than the previous questions.

"Wilder," said the professor. "Explain how we can hear a sound from around the corner of a building."

Olivia nodded. "The sound waves spread out as they pass the edge of the building. It's called diffraction."

"Correct."

Professor Cotton continued directing questions back and forth. Chad Newsome got the hardest question of the fourth round.

"Hawthorne," said the professor, looking at Chad. "Frost doesn't occur under cars, benches, and trees. Explain that phenomenon."

Chad sat forward in his seat, then back. He shook his head and looked over at Jerry and Brenda.

"Can any of your teammates answer?" the professor asked.

Brenda shook her head and gazed wide-eyed at Jerry.

His heart racing, Jerry cleared his throat and answered slowly. "Frost comes from atmospheric water vapor settling onto subfreezing surfaces on very calm, cold nights. All objects give off radiation.

Frost doesn't occur in the places you mentioned because the radiation is reflected by these overhead objects—sort of like a greenhouse—and prevents more cooling. The air underneath is kept a little warmer because the radiation can't escape like it can in open places."

Professor Cotton smiled. "Correct."

Kat, Kim, and Chad sat forward and grinned at Jerry, their thumbs up. "All right!" they whispered. Brenda squeezed Jerry's hand. A few people in the audience clapped.

Jerry couldn't help wishing that Cinnamon had been here to watch him save the point for his team.

The students answered the next few questions correctly, though everyone seemed to be holding their breath. The questions kept getting harder!

"Wilder," said Professor Cotton. "Explain Newton's first law regarding motion."

Jerry and Brenda grinned at each other. That was one of the questions they had worked on together.

Olivia sat tall in her chair, her nose in the air. "It says that a body tends to stay at rest or in uniform motion until an outside force acts on it."

Jerry sighed. Olivia *would* have to know that one.

"Correct. Hawthorne, please explain Newton's second law of motion."

Jerry had to smile. He'd answered this question, too, in his practice with Brenda. "It explains what happens when a force is applied to an object. The greater the force, the greater the acceleration of that object. The greater the mass of the object, the smaller the acceleration."

"Good. Wilder, it's your turn," said Professor Cotton. "Please explain why Newton's second law is not always clearly shown in motions that occur in the real world."

The boy sitting next to Olivia on the Wilder team said something like "Sheesh!" and people in the audience laughed. "I didn't even know what Newton's second law *was!*" he said.

The professor smiled. "Can anyone on the Wilder team answer the question?"

Everyone looked at Olivia. She shrugged.

"The question now goes to the Hawthorne team," said the professor. "Can anyone answer the question? For the game: Why is Newton's second law not always clearly shown in motions that occur in the real world?"

Jerry raised his hand and the professor nodded.

"It's because of friction," Jerry said.

"Can you explain further?"

"Well, any motion is opposed by a contact force. That's friction. Friction is hard to measure while you're measuring the other forces that cause the motion. Because of friction, it seems that a mass requires more force than is actually necessary for acceleration."

"Excellent." The professor smiled and looked out at the audience. "We have a winner. Congratulations, Hawthorne Middle School!"

A cheer went up from the audience. By twos and threes, they rose to their feet, applauding Jerry's team. Jerry looked out over the audience and caught his breath. The blurry faces seemed to be looking at *him*!

Brenda whooped and leaped out of her chair. Jerry stood, grinning, and he and Brenda slapped hands. He laughed while Chad and the Henley sisters thumped him on the back.

Jerry squinted into the audience as the house lights came up. His gaze stopped on Tony, who stood in the second row with a few other kids, smiling broadly. Jerry was startled to see him. Tony must have been surprised, too, to see Jerry up there on the stage. Jerry had lied to him about being on the science team. But if Tony was mad about that, he certainly didn't look it.

Maybe it was okay that Tony was here. Maybe he'd tell Cinnamon how Jerry had won the competition for Hawthorne.

Jerry soaked it all up: the applause, the cheering, the excitement. He'd never felt so good. Dozens of hands waved at him. He continued to grin, and he waved back, laughing.

# Chapter Fifteen

For the next hour, Jerry's heart continued to soar. He paced around his room, replaying the competition over and over in his head, relishing the feelings their victory had given him.

Jerry even imagined that Cinnamon had been very impressed with him while he was onstage and that this evening at the carnival, she would gaze into his eyes and say something wonderful like, "Jerry, you're so smart. I *love* smart guys."

But as the time for the carnival drew near, Jerry's fantasy about Cinnamon faded, and he began feeling very nervous. Maybe she hadn't been impressed with him. Maybe she'd decided that he was a dork, and maybe she and Gabe would "forget" to meet him at the Ferris wheel as they had planned. Maybe they would make fun of him for being on the science team.

Jerry put on his cool torn jeans and a long-sleeved T-shirt and came down the stairs. He checked his watch. He had exactly twenty-two minutes to walk to the high school and meet Cinnamon and the others at the Ferris wheel.

The doorbell rang. Jerry turned to peer through the screen at a man standing on the front porch. He lived across the street, but they had never spoken. Jerry didn't even know his name.

"Hi," Jerry said, hoping whatever the man wanted wouldn't take long. He didn't want to be late for the carnival. "Can I help you?"

"You can give me my newspaper back, that's what you can do!" the man yelled.

"What do you mean?"

"Don't you have eyes?" The man pointed to his feet.

On the stoop lay a large pile of newspapers, each paper neatly folded with a rubber band around it.

"Your dog's been running around the neighborhood, stealing them from porches!" the man cried. "I saw him with my own eyes. You should keep your dog at home where he belongs!" The man leaned down, grabbed one of the papers, and hurried off, mumbling to himself.

"Oh, no."

**137**

Jerry felt a dead weight in his stomach. Sassy hadn't been transformed after all. She was still the mischievous, dopey troublemaker she'd always been.

And maybe he hadn't transformed himself either, Jerry thought. Maybe he was really just a dork in disguise. Maybe the carnival would be a disaster.

The phone rang, and moments later, Mrs. Flack rushed down the stairs. "Jerry, Mrs. Whittaker from next door just called. She's very angry. Sassy took her newspaper."

"She's stolen papers from all over the neighborhood," Jerry said, pointing to the pile on the porch.

"Oh my gosh," his mother said. "Jerry, you're going to have to get those papers back to wherever they came from."

"I can't, Mom!" Jerry said, panic rising in his throat. "I'm meeting friends at the carnival in—" He checked his watch. "In nineteen and a half minutes."

"Not until every one of these papers is returned," Mrs. Flack said. "And put Sassy inside so she doesn't steal any more!"

Jerry stared at the large pile of newspapers. Sassy had stolen at least a dozen! He'd never get to the carnival in time to meet everybody. He'd have to call Cinnamon and explain why he was going to be late.

He rushed into the kitchen and looked up Cinnamon's phone number. His heart thumping, he dialed her house.

*Be there*, he thought. What if she had already left?

A young voice answered.

"Hi," Jerry said, breathlessly. "Is Cinnamon there, please?"

"Nope," said the voice.

"Are you her sister?" Jerry asked.

"Yes, *unfortunately*."

"Has Cinnamon already left to go to the carnival?" Jerry asked. "Or did she go to Robin's house?"

There was a loud sigh. "You sure ask a lot of questions."

"Just tell me, please," Jerry said urgently. "I'm supposed to meet her there, but something's come up. Do you know where I can find her?"

"Hey, my third-favorite TV show is on, you know? I gotta go." There was a pause and another loud sigh. "But she went to the carnival, if you *must* know."

The line went dead.

Jerry hung up. Maybe Cinnamon *had* decided that he was a dork, someone she didn't want to be seen with. Maybe she left early to meet her friends so she wouldn't have to hang around with him.

He'd just have to go late and look for them when he got there.

*   *   *

Jerry arrived at the high school an hour later. The place was hardly recognizable. The student parking lot was crowded with game booths, a Ferris wheel, a merry-go-round, and food stands selling hot dogs, soda, and cotton candy. Overhead, streamers, pennants, and colored lights—which hadn't yet been turned on—were strung between tall poles.

Jerry knew it was going to be very hard to find Cinnamon and the others. The carnival was packed with people. Most of them were middle school and high school students, but there were also plenty of little kids, parents, and even some grandparents. It was too crowded to move fast.

Jerry scanned the blurry mob for Cinnamon. She was probably off having fun with Robin, Tony, Craig . . . and Gabe. He had to find her!

"Hey, Jerry." Jerry turned to see Mr. Hooten. He stopped as the crowd passed, his wife at his side and his little boy riding on his shoulders.

Jerry grinned. "Hi."

"Having fun?" Mr. Hooten asked, smiling.

"Yeah," Jerry said.

Mr. Hooten introduced his wife and son, Joey. "You guys knocked my socks off at the competition," he said. "How did you know the answer to that last question?"

"I built a hovercraft with a vacuum cleaner

motor," Jerry said. "It demonstrates Newton's second law."

"I've read about those hovercrafts," Mr. Hooten said. "Is it finished?"

"Yeah."

"Great," said Mr. Hooten. "Why don't you bring it to school Monday? We'll give the class a demonstration."

"It's very loud," Jerry said. "You'd hear it all over the school."

"I'll warn the other teachers," Mr. Hooten said, grinning. "And Mr. Meyer."

"Okay," Jerry said. It was hard to believe that he'd be allowed to make that much noise during school.

Jerry said good-bye to Mr. Hooten and his family and set out to look for Cinnamon again. He circled the carnival three times before he saw her.

Cupid himself couldn't have timed it better. Just as the colored lights winked on overhead, the crowd parted and Jerry caught sight of Cinnamon. She stood talking with Robin, Craig, Tony . . . and Gabe.

She had never looked so beautiful, Jerry thought. She was wearing blue jeans and a hunter-green polo shirt that looked wonderful with the deep red hair that tumbled over her shoulders. With her dangly gold and green earrings, she reminded him of a Christmas package.

His heart hammered a staccato rhythm in his

chest, and he felt a goofy grin spread across his face. He immediately caught himself and straightened his lips into a horizontal line, so he wouldn't look like a geek.

He just hoped she'd still speak to him, now that she knew his secret.

He walked over to her and tapped her on the shoulder. She turned to him and beamed.

"Jerry!" she cried, squeezing his arm. "Where *were* you? We waited and waited! Didn't we, Gabe?"

"Yeah, for a minute," Gabe said, looking irritated.

"Hey, Flack, you made it," Craig said, gesturing with a jumbo-size cup of soda.

Robin scowled at him, but Tony said, "Hi, Jerry," and smiled.

"Hi." Jerry sighed with relief. Cinnamon was glad to see him! He felt uncomfortable, though, about Tony and how he'd lied to him about the science team. Jerry wondered if he would say anything about it.

But Tony just smiled and said nothing.

"Have you been on the Ferris wheel yet, Jerry?" Cinnamon asked.

"No," Jerry said. "I just got here. Sorry I'm late."

"Well, come on," Cinnamon said. "Let's all get a ride." Gabe groaned. "Oh, come on! It'll be fun."

Cinnamon and Robin led the way. Jerry strolled alongside Craig, watching Cinnamon's red hair bounce as she walked and talked animatedly with

Robin. He'd been doing his cool walk long enough that he didn't even have to think about it anymore. He was on automatic pilot now, strutting along in front of the master strutter, Gabe Marshall.

At the Ferris wheel, they stood in line for ten minutes to buy a ticket, then waited their turn.

A sign tacked up next to the Ferris wheel said ONLY TWO PEOPLE PER SEAT.

"Okay, who's going to sit with who?" Cinnamon called out.

Gabe shrugged, so Jerry did, too, but he was hoping he might get a chance to ride with Cinnamon.

When the Ferris wheel stopped, the line moved forward as the people in front of them got their seats.

Gabe walked up and stood next to Cinnamon, obviously putting himself in a position to ride with her.

But Cinnamon did a very surprising thing. Jerry watched her inch backward till she stood next to him. Robin got on the Ferris wheel, and Gabe was next in line.

"Come on," said the man who was seating the riders. He waved impatiently at Gabe.

Gabe looked around and realized he would have to ride with Robin. He scowled and slid in next to her.

"I guess we're next, Jerry," Cinnamon said.

**143**

Jerry's heart leaped as he and Cinnamon climbed into the seat. He couldn't believe it. He was sitting with Cinnamon O'Brien, the prettiest girl at the whole carnival.

The Ferris wheel turned a notch, and Craig and Tony got on. Jerry sat in the gently rocking seat and looked around him.

When the ride began, Cinnamon turned to him and said, "This is nothing compared to a great roller coaster, but it's still fun."

"Yeah."

This was it; he was alone with Cinnamon. And the best part was that *she had chosen him.* She didn't think he was a dork! His dreams had come true. What would he do now? What could he say to her?

Their seat cleared the top of the Ferris wheel's circle, and headed down. Jerry's stomach lifted, and Cinnamon giggled.

Gabe turned to look back at them, and what luck. It was at that moment that Cinnamon slid closer to Jerry and beamed at him.

"I love that feeling when we come over the top," Cinnamon said.

Jerry laughed, thrilled at her closeness.

Gabe scowled and turned forward again.

Jerry shivered just a tiny bit with nervousness and stretched his arm along the back of the seat. He wasn't exactly putting his arm around Cinnamon, but it was the next best thing. Cinnamon inched closer to him, and her arm rested against his chest.

Jerry drew in a breath. *They were touching.* He wished the ride would go on and on—for months, even. He wouldn't need food or water or sleep. He would just sit here and enjoy the excitement of having her arm resting against him.

Cinnamon waved at some friends on the ground and once at Gabe, who scowled and turned away. She smiled and leaned closer to Jerry.

"Gabe and I saw you today at that thing," Cinnamon said.

"What thing?" Jerry asked, knowing exactly what she meant.

"You were on the stage, and some old guy was asking you questions."

"Oh, you mean the science competition." Jerry shrugged as if it didn't matter.

"Yeah, Gabe and I came to watch them set up the carnival and came inside for a drink," Cinnamon said. She wrinkled her nose. "You really *like* science?"

"Not too much," Jerry lied, then thought better of it. "Well, I do like it better than some other subjects." He watched her face and added, "We won the competition."

"I think science is boring," Cinnamon said.

"Oh." Jerry wasn't surprised, but he was still disappointed to hear her say it. And she sure didn't seem to care that his team had won.

"Well," he said. "I guess not everybody thinks

science is interesting. Depends on your point of view, I guess."

"I don't see how *anybody* can like it," Cinnamon said. "I practically fall asleep in science class. I keep watching the clock, waiting for it to get over with!"

How could anyone fall asleep in science class? Jerry wondered.

He gazed out over the crowd below. He spotted a red sweatshirt and realized it was Brenda. He smiled and leaned forward to watch her.

Brenda was walking along with Kim, Kat, and Chad. They all carried paper cones of cotton candy. Brenda said something that made everyone laugh, and she grinned. Brenda was good at making people laugh, Jerry thought. She had a great sense of humor.

Jerry suddenly felt a little sorry for himself. He was missing out on the fun with Brenda and the others.

The impact of that thought was staggering. *I'm with Cinnamon O'Brien!* he reminded himself. This was the moment he'd been waiting for!

"Who're you looking at?" Cinnamon asked, leaning forward. "Oh, it's *Brenda*, right?" She said the name as if it were a bad word.

"Yeah," Jerry said. "She's down there with the science team."

"Geez, Jerry," Cinnamon said, "Brenda's such a geek. How come you like to hang out with her and the rest of those nerds, anyway?"

A hot surge of anger washed over Jerry, startling him. "Brenda's not a geek," he said, his voice suddenly loud. "She's very nice, and so are her friends."

Cinnamon shrugged. "If you like that type," she said. The Ferris wheel began to slow. "Oh, look, the ride's over."

Their seat was the last to stop at the bottom. The Ferris wheel man unlatched the safety bar in front of them, and Jerry and Cinnamon climbed out.

He'd had his few minutes alone with Cinnamon, but it sure hadn't been what he'd hoped for. They'd spent most of the time talking about how boring science was. And he felt bad about how Cinnamon put Brenda down. How could anyone be mean about Brenda? Brenda was so much fun, and she was nice to everybody.

Jerry and Cinnamon walked a few steps away and joined the others.

He glanced at Cinnamon, suddenly puzzled. He couldn't believe he wasn't having the time of his life. She seemed to like him. This was what he'd been working for since school started.

"What now?" Robin asked. She had her usual crabby expression on her face. Jerry wondered why Cinnamon liked being around her. He couldn't stand Robin himself.

"Come on," Cinnamon said, grinning. "Let's just walk. We'll see and be seen."

"Cool," Craig said, and Tony grinned.

They walked in a group along the fairway.

"Oooo, look at the cute stuffed animals!" Cinnamon squealed. She pointed to a furry rabbit and a fluffy kitten in the booth closest to her.

Craig swallowed some soda and turned to Cinnamon. "You have to throw a ball and hit those moving targets. Then you get a stuffed animal."

"Win one for me, you guys," Cinnamon said. She stood and looked back and forth between Gabe and Jerry. "I really, really want a stuffed animal for my room. You know, to remember the carnival."

"You won't remember it otherwise?" Robin asked sarcastically.

"Not as well," Cinnamon said, smiling. "Come on, guys. Win me one."

"Yeah, come on," Craig said, looking from Gabe to Jerry. "Let's see which of you dudes can win a prize for Cinnamon."

Gabe eyed the row of cardboard squirrels moving quickly along the back of the stand.

"I can hit one of those easy," he said.

"You gotta hit three, kid," said a man with greased-back hair and tattoos on both hairy arms. He stood behind the counter in the booth, a cigarette dangling from his lips, and he squinted at them through a haze of drifting smoke. "And you gotta buy a ticket."

"Okay," Gabe said. He handed his money to the man, who gave him four balls.

"Four chances to hit three squirrels," the man said.

"Easy," Gabe murmured.

The man smirked, leaned against the end of the counter and folded his arms.

"You can do it, Gabe," Tony said.

Gabe stood a moment, watching the marching squirrels.

"Win me something, Gabe," Cinnamon urged.

"Okay, okay," Gabe said, irritated. "Just let me concentrate, will ya?"

Cinnamon and Robin laughed behind their hands but kept quiet.

Jerry watched Gabe and realized with interest that his cool manner was gone. Even Gabe could get nervous.

Gabe slowly picked up a ball. He watched the squirrels a moment, wound up, and threw the first ball. A squirrel toppled over.

Craig and Tony whooped.

"Yay!" Cinnamon squealed. "Good throw, Gabe!"

Gabe picked up the next ball, focused on his target, and threw. He missed.

Was it Jerry's imagination, or had the squirrels moved a little faster the exact moment the ball had left Gabe's hand?

"Oh, no!" Cinnamon cried. "You can't miss again."

Gabe scowled at her. "I know, okay? I *know*."

Craig snorted, and Robin laughed.

Jerry kept his eyes focused on the squirrels. Gabe took a big breath, wound up, and threw. He knocked down a second squirrel.

"Another squirrel bites the dust," Tony said.

Cinnamon jumped up and down, clapping. "Fantastic!"

Jerry had been right. The squirrels had suddenly moved faster when Gabe threw the ball. The man in the booth had to be controlling it, Jerry thought. The guy hadn't moved from his place at the far edge of the counter since they had all approached the booth.

"Now just one more," Cinnamon said. "Do it for me, Gabe. Knock down one more."

"Just a minute," Jerry said, holding up his hand. "Would you do us a favor?" he asked the man in the booth. "Would you stand over there, please?"

He pointed to the other side of the booth.

The man's lip curled, and he eyed Jerry keenly. "What's your problem, kid?" he asked.

"The game is rigged. You're making the squirrels move faster," Jerry said. "There must be a button down there, and you're pushing against it with your knee. So move over to the other side."

"I think you kids would have more fun somewhere else," the man said, scowling. He threw Gabe's money back on the counter. "Go on, get out of here."

"Hey!" Gabe said. "I want to take my last throw."

"I said, get out of here," the man said. "I gave you your money back. *Scram!*"

He turned away from them and walked to the back of the booth.

"Jerry!" Cinnamon whined. "Look what you did! Gabe was about to win me a stuffed animal."

"Yeah," Gabe said. "I coulda won it easy! I only had to knock down one more squirrel."

"He was cheating!" Jerry said, baffled at their reaction. Why weren't they thanking him?

"I was hitting them, wasn't I?" Gabe said.

"Yeah, he was hitting them, even though the guy was cheating!" Cinnamon said. "And now I don't get my stuffed animal!"

Craig spoke up. "I think we'd better show that guy what we think of his cheating us."

He hurled his big cup of soda at the squirrels, which were still marching in a line across the little stage. The soda splashed all over the squirrels and ran down the cardboard flat surrounding them.

"Hey, what're you doin'?" the carnival man yelled.

"Knock it off, Craig!" Jerry hollered.

"Oh, so now you're *defending* the guy who cheated us?" Gabe shouted, backing quickly away from the booth. The others followed him.

"Come on, Jerry!" Cinnamon called to him. "That guy deserved what Craig did!"

Jerry, who moments ago had felt virtuous for stopping the carnival man from cheating them, now felt guilty for pointing out the con and starting all this trouble.

"Sorry," Jerry said to carnival man.

Cinnamon rushed to him, grabbed his arm, and dragged him away.

Music began playing on the other side of the crowd.

"Come on, Jerry, the dance has started," Cinnamon said. "I might not be able to get the stuffed animal, but I can *dance*! Let's go."

Jerry let Cinnamon take him back to the others, a gloomy feeling settling into his chest. This evening wasn't at all what he'd expected. He thought if Cinnamon didn't reject him, he'd have a great time. But he was miserable. It didn't even matter that Cinnamon liked him.

They all followed Cinnamon as she led them to the area that had been cleared for the dance in front of a small makeshift stage.

Three guitar players and a drummer were performing a song with a driving beat.

"Who are these guys?" Jerry asked Cinnamon.

"They're called Otis Wants Bread," Cinnamon said. "They're starting to get famous. They have a CD and everything."

They stood and listened, and Jerry found himself scanning the crowd for Brenda and his science team friends. He wondered what they were doing now.

He almost wished now that he'd come with Brenda instead. It was weird to realize that after all he'd been through to be accepted by the cool kids, they just weren't fun.

His gaze drifted back to the dance area. Kids were starting to dance now. His face heated up just thinking about dancing. He'd never danced in his life!

Cinnamon pulled on Gabe's arm, and they walked out in front of the stage and began to dance. Jerry watched, feeling glad that Cinnamon hadn't pulled *him* out there. Gabe looked pretty good dancing. Jerry was sure *he* wouldn't look good, and he didn't want to try it for the first time in front of anybody. He wanted to practice in front of the mirror at home.

Craig nudged Robin, and they started dancing. Tony walked over to stand next to Jerry.

"I saw you in the science competition." Tony had to shout to be heard over the band.

"Oh, yeah," Jerry shouted back, feeling the heat in his face. "Sorry I told you I wasn't on the team. I thought you might think . . . well . . ." He shrugged.

"I know," Tony said. "It's okay."

They listened to the music some more.

Then Tony leaned over again. "You think I could be on the team?" he said loud in Jerry's ear.

Jerry turned to gawk at him. "You mean, the *science* team?"

"Yeah," Tony said. This time, it was Tony whose face turned red. "You think I could be on it? I kind of like science."

Jerry laughed. "*Yeah*," he said. "Yeah, that would be great. Want me to tell Mr. Hooten you're interested?"

Tony smiled, relief spreading across his face. "Okay, cool. You meet on Tuesdays, right?"

"Right," Jerry said, grinning.

He couldn't believe it. One of the cool kids liked science too. Amazing.

The song ended, and the crowd clapped for the band. Cinnamon, Gabe, Craig, and Robin returned.

The music changed now to a slow song. Cinnamon looked over at Jerry and cocked her head at him. "Want to dance?" she asked.

For weeks, Jerry had dreamed of this moment. But now he didn't feel thrilled. He shrugged.

"Sure, let's dance," he said.

Jerry followed Cinnamon into the crowd of dancers.

She stepped up to Jerry and wrapped her arms around him.

Jerry's body quivered. It *was* a nice feeling, he decided.

She's going to feel my heart slamming against her, he thought. She's going to feel me shake.

He took her in his arms. Their cheeks touched, and his nose almost brushed her ear. Her hair smelled like fresh apples.

Her face felt cool and soft against his. Under his hands, her waist, small and curved, moved slightly as she rocked with him back and forth.

Jerry settled into a kind of dream state and found himself thinking of Brenda. It would be fun to dance with Brenda, he thought. She'd probably say something funny, and they'd both end up laughing.

"Jerry," Cinnamon said in a low voice.

"Hmm?"

"Is Gabe watching us?" she asked.

"Gabe?"

"Yeah," she said. "I was just wondering if Gabe's mad because I asked you to slow dance."

"Oh." Jerry squinted at the edge of the crowd where Gabe stood with Craig, Robin, and Tony. Gabe had turned his back on them, talking with the others.

"I don't know," Jerry said. "I can't see his face. Do you want him to be mad?"

Cinnamon giggled. "It's kind of fun to make him jealous sometimes." She pulled away a little and looked Jerry in the face. "Oh, but I'm having a good time with you, too, Jerry."

Sure, Jerry thought. But you're thinking of Gabe. And I'm thinking about Brenda.

Jerry's gaze moved to a figure across the dance area. He thought it was Brenda, but he squinted to be sure.

He was right. Brenda stood with Kim, Kat, and Chad, and she didn't seem to know he was there. She was laughing at something.

Good old Brenda. Good old smart, funny Brenda.

He made up his mind, and his decision didn't even surprise him. It felt right.

The slow song ended, and Jerry walked with Cinnamon to join Gabe and the others.

"I'm going to go hang out with Brenda," he told them.

*"What?"* Cinnamon said, her eyes big.

"Yeah," Jerry said.

Gabe smirked, and Robin stared at him in disbelief.

"See you guys," Jerry said. "Thanks for the dance, Cinnamon."

"Sure," Cinnamon said in a small voice.

Jerry turned and started across the dance area.

The band began to play again, and the dance area became crowded. Jerry elbowed his way over to where Brenda stood. She turned and watched him approach.

"Hi," Jerry said to her, suddenly feeling a little shy.

"Hey, Flack," she said. "Having fun?"

"Probably not as much fun as you," Jerry said.

Brenda looked surprised. "How come?"

Jerry shrugged and grinned. "Oh, I guess I don't have as much in common with those guys."

"What a shock," Brenda said.

"You guys are a lot cooler," Jerry said. "Tony's different, though. He wants to join the science team."

Brenda grinned. "Great."

"So can I hang out with you guys?" Jerry asked.

Brenda shrugged. "Sure." She looked at Kim and Kat and Chad, who were all smiling. "What do you guys want to do now?"

"Have you been on the Ferris wheel yet?" Jerry asked.

"Not yet," Kim and Kat said at the same time.

"Want to give it a whirl?" Jerry asked Brenda.

"Sure!" Brenda said. "I love Ferris wheels."

"Great. Let's go," Jerry said.

Jerry and his science team friends grinned and headed for the Ferris wheel.

And Jerry knew that *this* Ferris wheel ride was going to be very cool.

# Chapter Sixteen

"Hey, Jerry, you got glasses," Tony said, grinning. "They look good."

It was the beginning of science class, and Jerry was setting up the hovercraft.

"Thanks," Jerry said. "It's pretty cool being able to see."

The bell rang, and everybody went to their seats.

"Jerry, are you ready to show us your special project?" Mr. Hooten asked.

"Yes," Jerry said. He tapped his glasses up on his nose and walked to the front of the class. He stopped in front of the hovercraft, which leaned against the wall.

"What is it?" asked Kim Henley.

"It's a hovercraft," Jerry said. "The craft itself is made from this piece of wood." He rolled the wooden circle forward and explained how it worked.

"Show them," said Brenda.

Jerry sat in the middle of the wooden disk and nodded to Mr. Hooten, who plugged in the vacuum cleaner motor.

It roared to life. The kids rose from their seats, some covering their ears, as Jerry was lifted an inch off the floor.

Jerry turned off the motor. "That's how it works," he said. "If we had more room, you could see Newton's second law in action."

"Oh, but we have the whole length of the hall-way," said Mr. Hooten with a grin. "I have some long extension cords. Come on. I warned the teachers."

Jerry beamed. "Great!"

He and Mr. Hooten led the class into the hall.

"One end of this rope is attached to the hovercraft," Jerry said. "We'll attach the other end to this spring scale." He held up a tubular device. "The person pulling the hovercraft pulls on the spring scale and the pointer registers how many newtons of force are being used."

"We'll give you a ride first, Jerry," said Mr. Hooten. He had already plugged in the extension cords. "Hop on."

Jerry sat in the middle of the disk and grabbed hold of the metal handles.

Mr. Hooten plugged in the motor. "We'll try forty newtons of force. Ready?"

"Ready," Jerry said, grinning. He flipped on the motor; the sound echoed off the walls and ceiling and made even more noise than it had in the classroom. One by one, classroom doors opened down the hall and students peered out to see what was causing the blast.

Mr. Hooten told Brenda to hold on to the hovercraft. Holding the spring scale and watching the pointer, he pulled on the hovercraft while Brenda held on.

When the pointer reached forty newtons, Mr. Hooten nodded to Brenda, and she let go. Mr. Hooten slowly backed up, keeping the pointer steady, and pulled Jerry with him.

The constant force caused them to quickly pick up speed. Jerry's hair fluttered and his shirt flapped on his back. He whooped and laughed as he flew down the hall behind Mr. Hooten. The kids in the hallway and in the classroom doorways cheered and clapped.

Mr. Hooten slowed and stopped when they ran out of extension cord and Jerry drifted past him and jerked to a stop at the end of the rope. He turned off the motor.

"Man, that was fun!"

Then the hall filled with students who piled out of their classrooms to surround Jerry on his hovercraft.

"Jerry! That's so cool! Where did you get it?"

Jerry heard Cinnamon's voice in the noisy clamor around him. He looked up into her eyes. She and Gabe stood right beside him.

"I built it," Jerry said.

Cinnamon's eyes got big and she knelt next to him. *"Really?"*

"I'll have to build one sometime," Gabe said.

Cinnamon rolled her eyes. She smiled and put a hand on Jerry's arm.

Mr. Hooten gently pushed his way through the crowd. "I pulled with a force of forty newtons," he said. "If I had pulled with ten newtons, do you think Jerry would have had such a fast ride?"

"No!" shouted the kids.

"What else was a factor in how fast Jerry's ride was?"

"His weight," Brenda said at the edge of the crowd.

"Right," Mr. Hooten said. "If I pulled someone my size with a force of forty newtons, would the ride be as fast as Jerry's was?"

"No," the kids called out.

"How about a ride for us, Mr. Hooten?" asked Brenda. That suggestion was met with loud cheers.

"If it's okay with Jerry and the other teachers,"

Mr. Hooten said, glancing between Jerry and his colleagues.

"Sure," Jerry said. The teachers nodded.

Mr. Hooten laughed. "Okay, everyone, let's have fun with physics!"

After school, Jerry went back to Mr. Hooten's classroom to pack up his hovercraft. Mr. Landau, the school custodian, walked up and down the aisles between the desks, mopping the floor.

"Jerry, I'm going to make a phone call," Mr. Hooten said. "Do you need help with the hovercraft?"

"Would it be okay if I left it here tonight? My mom'll pick me up tomorrow. I'll take it then."

"Okay," Mr. Hooten said. "I'll be back by the time Mr. Landau is finished in here, and I'll lock the room."

"Great."

"That was an excellent project," Mr. Hooten said. "And it certainly was a hit with the students."

Jerry grinned. "Thanks."

Mr. Hooten smiled and left.

Jerry pulled the hovercraft away from the wall.

"Congratulations, Jerry." He looked up to see Brenda standing in the doorway.

"Thanks," Jerry said. "It really worked great."

"I mean congratulations for everything." Brenda walked into the classroom. "For winning the science competition, for building the hovercraft, and for wow-ing every kid in school. Even Cinnamon O'Brien was impressed with science for once."

"Yeah," Jerry said, grinning. "I guess she found out science isn't *always* boring."

Jerry gazed at Brenda. "You want to take a ride on the hovercraft with me?"

"At the same time?"

"Sure."

"There isn't much room."

"I know," Jerry said. "You'll have to sit on my lap."

"Okay."

"Mr. Landau," Jerry said, "would you mind giving us a shove?"

"Sure."

Jerry plugged in the extension cord and sat in the middle of the wooden disk. Brenda sat on his lap. She was right—there wasn't much room.

"Push, Mr. Landau," Jerry said. He turned on the motor and grabbed the handles as it roared to life.

Mr. Landau ran along behind the hovercraft, pushing Jerry's back. He gave one final shove that sent Jerry and Brenda zooming down the hall alone.

Brenda threw her head back to feel the breeze in her face, and her hair flew into Jerry's mouth. Jerry let go of a handle to brush it away. The hovercraft started to spin, and he lost his balance.

Jerry and Brenda tumbled off the hovercraft and lay in a heap on the floor, laughing. Jerry reached over to the extension cord and pulled it out of the socket. The hovercraft had traveled halfway down the hall.

"That was so much fun," Brenda said, laughing.

Jerry glanced back down the hall. Mr. Landau gave them a wave and returned to the classroom; the hall was empty.

Jerry crawled over to Brenda. She looked pretty, her hair messed up and her eyes crinkling with laughter. Before he lost his nerve, he leaned over and kissed her. She was still laughing, and he planted the kiss right on her teeth.

"Hey," Brenda said. "I wasn't ready. Try it again."

Jerry kissed her a second time.

"There, that's better," she said, smiling. "That was really cool."

"What?" Jerry asked. "The hovercraft ride or the—the kiss?"

Brenda laughed. "Both. But why wouldn't they be? They both came from a pretty cool person."

"Really?" Jerry asked. He sat back on the floor. "You think I'm cool now?"

"Definitely," Brenda said. "But you were always cool. You just needed a few lessons on how to *project* it."

"Thanks," Jerry said. "You're very cool, too."

Brenda smiled. "It takes one to know one."

Jerry grinned back and got to his feet. "Come on, Bren," he said. "I'll walk you home."